Nightmare Mountain

Nightmare Mountain

Peg Kehret

COBBLEHILL BOOKS/Dutton   New York

Copyright © 1989 by Peg Kehret

Library of Congress Cataloging-in-Publication Data
Kehret, Peg.
    Nightmare mountain / Peg Kehret.
        p.   cm.
    Summary: Twelve-year-old Molly's visit to her aunt and uncle's llama ranch in
the state of Washington leads her into unexpected danger and suspense.
    ISBN 0-525-65008-3
    [1. Mystery and detective stories. 2. Ranch life—Washington (State)
3. Llamas—Fiction.] I. Title.
PZ7.K2518Ni   1989
[Fic]—dc19   89-1535
                                                                       CIP
                                                                        AC

Published in the United States by Cobblehill Books,
an affiliate of Dutton Children's Books,
a division of Penguin Books USA Inc.
375 Hudson Street, New York, New York 10014

Designer: Jean Krulis
Printed in the United States of America
First edition   10 9 8 7 6 5 4

For Ginny and Bob Bither

Nightmare Mountain

One

Dear Mom:

Someone's trying to kill me. It's too complicated to explain in a letter but will you cut your trip short so I can come home?

Aunt Karen's worse and Uncle Phil is staying at the hospital with her, so they can't help. I think Glendon might be the one who's after me.

Please hurry.

Love,
Molly

P.S. This is no joke.

Two

Molly wondered what Glendon would be like. She'd seen pictures of him and she knew he was twelve years old, the same as she was, but she didn't know much else about him.

Although it was six years since her Aunt Karen eloped with Phil Baldwin, Molly had never met Phil or his son. She hoped she would like Glendon. If he was fun to be with, she would have a great time during her month at the llama ranch. If he was a nerd . . . well, Molly wasn't even going to consider that possibility. Think positive. That's what her mom always said.

When Molly got off the plane at the Seattle airport, Aunt Karen was waiting. She looked just the way Molly remembered her—tall and slim and smiling.

"This," Aunt Karen said, when she finally quit hugging Molly, "is your Uncle Phil."

Molly looked up at the biggest man she'd ever seen. He wore a red-and-black-plaid wool shirt, jeans, and brown leather work boots. He had a thick, bushy beard and he towered over Aunt Karen.

"How do you do," Molly said, and held out her hand.

"None of that formal how-do-you-do business with me, Molly Neuman," he said, and he threw his huge arms around Molly, lifted her right off her feet, and gave her a bear hug. His beard prickled the skin on her face but she laughed and hugged him back.

"Put her down," said Aunt Karen. "She isn't a baby to be dandled in the air. You'll embarrass her."

"What?" roared Uncle Phil. "No female is ever embarrassed when a man wants to hug her. Isn't that so, Molly?" He winked at her, as he put her back on her feet.

Molly winked back at him and he grinned. She knew she was going to like Uncle Phil.

"Why didn't you tell me she was beautiful?" Uncle Phil said. "Maybe I could have controlled myself if I had been prepared."

"Of course she's beautiful," Aunt Karen said. "She's my niece, isn't she? What did you expect?"

Molly knew she was not beautiful. She was a perfectly ordinary girl with short, straight brown hair, and braces on her teeth, and a tendency to be pudgier than she'd like. But listening to them talk like that made her feel good.

Molly was disappointed that Glendon wasn't at the airport.

"He's in school," Aunt Karen explained.

They drove north, nearly to the Canadian border, and then headed east. Molly, who had lived in Los Angeles all her life, marveled at all the trees. Everywhere she looked, it was green.

"Our ranch adjoins the North Cascades National Park," Aunt Karen said. "The original owners intended to build a ski resort but they ran out of money before the project was completed."

When the paved road ended, they continued on a narrow gravel lane that wound through groves of fir trees as it climbed higher. Molly pointed to white patches in the shaded areas of the forest.

"There's still snow," she said.

"The snow stays on Mount Baker all year round," Uncle Phil said. "You just have to climb higher to get to it in the summer than you do in the winter."

"Just beyond our ranch," Aunt Karen said, "the road ends and there's only a path on up the mountain."

"A path and our lift," Uncle Phil added. "There was a ski lift on the property and I've adapted it so we can carry supplies to the llamas during the summer months, when they're in the upper pasture. Most of the time, my truck will make it up the path but if we get a rainy spell, I have to use the lift."

"I've never seen a ski lift," Molly said. "I've only seen snow once before in my whole life."

"An underprivileged child," Uncle Phil said. "But we'll change that. There's still plenty of snow above our upper pasture."

"How deep does it get in winter?" Molly asked.

"Over your head," Uncle Phil said. "Over my head, too."

"Aren't you afraid it will bury your house?"

"The deep snow is farther up the mountain and it causes few problems. Once in awhile, a foolish hiker triggers a minor avalanche but mostly we just enjoy looking at it."

Molly hadn't expected to see snow in June. Maybe Glendon could teach her to ski.

The car bumped and bounced the last few miles. At last, they came to a gate across the road and Aunt Karen jumped out and held it open while Uncle Phil drove the car through.

"Our ranch is completely fenced, to keep the llamas in," Uncle Phil explained. "Even the upper pasture."

Molly peered out the window, eager for her first glimpse of a llama. "There's one now," she said. "There's a whole bunch of them!"

"Sixty, in all," Uncle Phil said. "Four more are already in the upper pasture for the summer and Merrylegs is in the barn. She's expecting her baby any day now so we have her in a pen where we can keep an eye on her."

"We'll be moving the rest of these up the mountain to the high pasture this week," Aunt Karen said. "Perhaps you'd like to help herd them."

"You bet!" She looked at the llamas' long, shaggy coats. "Do people buy them for their wool?" she asked.

"It would be much too expensive to have a llama only for the wool," Aunt Karen said. "Their wool is used for spinning but that isn't the main reason people buy them."

"A few are bought for pack animals," Uncle Phil said, "but most people want them for pets."

Molly imagined what the manager of her condo in Los Angeles would say if she asked to keep a llama in the courtyard.

It felt good to get out of the car and stretch her legs. The two-story gray house had an old-fashioned front porch, with a railing and a porch swing. The house would make a good collage, Molly thought. She'd use gray flannel for the house and strips of white felt for the porch.

Her hobby was making collages out of fabric scraps. Last year she won first prize at her school's Craft Show for a collage of the school library. She'd used dozens of tiny scraps, all in different colors, for the shelves of books.

Aunt Karen opened the front door and led Molly inside. They were welcomed by a big dog, which barked happily and licked their hands.

"This is Buckie," Aunt Karen said. "He's part collie and part German shepherd. He's had obedience training, so if he bothers you, tell him to *sit* and he'll mind."

"He won't bother me," Molly said. "I've always wanted a dog but our condo rules don't allow pets."

For an entire month, she could play with Buckie and brush him and take him for walks. This would be a great vacation!

Uncle Phil carried her bags up the stairs and down the hall to a small room at the back of the house.

"I'll unpack later," Molly said. "I want to go see the llamas first, and play with Buckie."

Uncle Phil laughed. "We'll give you a quick tour of the ranch before we go back to work," he said. "Then you can play with Buckie if you want, while we do our chores."

First they took her to the barn and introduced her to Merrylegs, the llama that was going to have a baby. Merrylegs was a shaggy, gentle creature whose eyes lit up when she saw Uncle Phil. He petted her and talked to her and Merrylegs responded with a soft, melodic noise.

"Llamas hum when they're contented," Uncle Phil said, "the way a cat purrs."

Molly reached up to pet Merrylegs' long neck. The gray fur felt thick and coarse.

Next they showed her the shed behind the house where they kept all their garden tools and supplies and then they walked out in the pasture to see the other llamas. These animals weren't as docile as Merrylegs and Molly couldn't get close enough to pet any of them, but they watched her carefully and seemed to be as curious about her as she was about them.

"Over there," Aunt Karen said, pointing to a huge field of pruned fir trees, "are our Christmas trees. Every December, we sell trees, to supplement our income from the llamas. Our customers chop their own, so the trees are always fresh and we never cut down more trees than we sell."

Molly thought that sounded like lots more fun than choosing a tree in the supermarket parking lot, the way she and Mom always did.

When it was time for Uncle Phil and Aunt Karen to get back to their work, Molly unpacked her things and then decided to play with Buckie.

She didn't see any dog toys so she got out her collage box. Buckie nudged her knee with his nose.

"Be patient," Molly said. "I'm getting you a toy." In

the bottom of the box was a small doll which she had made out of some scraps of corduroy. It had yellow yarn for hair, buttons for eyes, and an old sock for stuffing. She showed the doll to Buckie.

"This is Fifi," she said, as Buckie sniffed the doll. "Fifi."

She showed the doll to Buckie several times, each time repeating the name, Fifi, and letting Buckie smell the doll.

Then she shut Buckie out of the bedroom and put Fifi under the bed.

"Where's Fifi?" she asked Buckie, when she let him back in. "Go find Fifi."

Buckie caught on quickly and began sniffing everywhere, rushing around the room until he finally caught Fifi's scent. He poked his head under the bed, grabbed the doll in his mouth, and looked at Molly, wagging his tail triumphantly.

"Good dog," Molly said, as she took Fifi from him. "Good Buckie."

Next she took the doll downstairs, put Buckie outside, and hid the doll in the kitchen. When she let Buckie in again he searched until he found the doll. He carried Fifi to Molly and dropped the doll at her feet. Then he stood, looking expectant, as if to say, "Hurry and hide Fifi so I can find it again."

Molly enjoyed the game as much as Buckie did and

they played it until Glendon got home from school. She knew when he was coming because she heard Uncle Phil holler, "Glendon! There's a beautiful young lady here to see you." Molly ran out on the porch. She saw an orange school bus turn around at the end of the lane and head back toward town. Uncle Phil and Aunt Karen joined her and Aunt Karen put her arm around Molly's shoulders.

A solemn boy trudged toward the house. Molly smiled and waved at him, her eyes shining with excitement.

"Hurry and meet Molly," Uncle Phil said, when Glendon was nearly to the house.

"We've been telling her how glad we are that she's come," Aunt Karen said. "I'm tired of being the only female in this house." She smiled at Molly. "I always wanted a daughter," she said. "I think I'll pretend you're mine, while you're here."

Glendon stopped at the bottom of the porch steps. He didn't smile; he didn't say he was glad to see her. He just looked at her.

Molly stepped down and stood beside him. She was surprised to see that he was no taller than she was. Since Uncle Phil was so big, she'd expected his son to be tall, too. Glendon's brown hair was short and straight, like hers, and he also had braces on his teeth.

"Hi, cousin," Molly said. "We almost look like twins."

Glendon glared at her, as if she'd insulted him.

Her smile faded and she tried again. "I was sorry you

10

couldn't come to the airport," she said. "When does your school get out?"

"Next week."

"Mine, too. I had to take my final tests early."

Glendon didn't reply.

Maybe he's shy, Molly thought. Maybe it's hard for him to talk to people he doesn't know well. She tried to think of something more to say, to put him at ease.

"You kids have fun getting acquainted," Uncle Phil said. "I have work to do." He headed back toward the barn.

"I have to start dinner," Aunt Karen said. She went in to the kitchen, leaving Molly and Glendon to stare at each other.

"I didn't mind getting out early," Molly said. "And my teacher said this trip would be educational."

No answer. The silence seemed awkward to Molly but Glendon didn't appear to notice. He went inside, climbed the stairs to his room, and shut the door.

Molly wondered how long it would take for him to relax. She scratched Buckie's ears, picked up Fifi, and went upstairs to get the tin of cookies she'd brought along.

She sat in her room awhile, petting Buckie, and wishing Glendon would come out of his room. He didn't. Finally she took the cookies downstairs and gave them to Aunt Karen. "I made them myself," she said.

"What kind are they?"

"Basically, I used Mom's chocolate chip cookie recipe."

"What a treat. I remember her cookies but I seldom have time to bake desserts."

Molly could understand that. It took her one whole afternoon to bake these. She had intended to make chocolate chip cookies but after the batter was already mixed, she discovered they were out of chocolate chips so she used raisins and a bag of peanut M & Ms instead. She thought the result was better than the original recipe.

Glendon finally came downstairs at dinnertime. Aunt Karen dished up the food on each person's plate and carried the plates to the table. Molly gulped when she saw the generous servings of green beans and carrots on her plate. She hated vegetables, every kind except corn, but she'd promised her mother that she would eat whatever Aunt Karen and Uncle Phil served. She didn't want to break her promise at the very first meal.

"We grow all our own vegetables," Uncle Phil said, as if he could read her mind. "They're better than what you can buy."

"Also," Aunt Karen added, "I have a few food allergies, so our meals tend to be simple."

Molly tried to look enthusiastic. She was glad to see a hot turkey sandwich on her plate, along with the beans

12

and carrots. She put a large piece of bread on her fork and a tiny piece of carrot and then dipped both in the turkey gravy. Maybe the flavor of the bread and gravy would camouflage the carrots and she'd be able to eat them without gagging.

As she put the food in her mouth, she realized Glendon was watching her. She glanced at him but he quickly looked away. Molly wondered if he had guessed how much she disliked vegetables. Something in his expression made her suspect that he knew.

"I love turkey sandwiches," she said.

"Sometimes we have veggie dinners," Glendon said. "Three vegetables and that's all."

Molly looked closely at him. He was definitely smirking. For the first time, she had doubts about being away from home for an entire month.

The next morning, she was relieved to see that breakfast consisted of scrambled eggs and toast. After last night's conversation, she was afraid she might be expected to eat broccoli for breakfast. At home, she and Mom usually had cereal or else they ate leftovers from the night before. Molly's favorite breakfast was cold pizza.

Molly took her bottle of cod-liver-oil pills to the table with her. She opened it, removed one capsule, put the pill in her mouth and took a big gulp of orange juice to help her swallow it. It wasn't until she set the juice glass back down that she realized Glendon was staring at her again.

"What was that pill you took?" he asked. "Are you sick?"

Molly thought she detected a note of hope in the question. Maybe Glendon was wishing she would get sick and have to go back home.

"It was a cod-liver-oil pill," she explained. "I take one every morning and I promised Mom I wouldn't forget."

"Cod-liver oil! Yuck!" Glendon wrinkled up his nose.

"They aren't so bad," Molly said. "There's vitamin A in them and some other vitamin."

"We don't take vitamin pills," Glendon said.

"Mom thinks the cod-liver-oil pills help keep me healthy," Molly said. "I hardly ever catch cold."

"Then maybe Glendon should take them," Uncle Phil said. "He was sick all last winter."

Glendon glared at Molly again. Clearly, he thought cod-liver-oil pills were a horrible idea. No doubt he would blame her if his parents decided that he should take them.

"I don't know if they really help or not," Molly said.

"How many days of school did you miss this year because you were sick?" Uncle Phil asked.

"I didn't miss any," Molly said.

"There, you see?" Uncle Phil said. "Glendon was sick half a dozen times."

"I had chicken pox," Glendon said. "Cod-liver oil doesn't prevent chicken pox."

"Once, you had chicken pox. The rest of the time you had head colds."

Molly decided it might be wise to change the subject.

"Buckie slept in my room last night," she said.

"Dogs can always tell when someone likes them," Aunt Karen said. "He'll probably want to sleep in your room the whole time you're here."

"No, he won't," Glendon said. "He wants to sleep in my room but I forgot and shut my door last night." He glared at Molly, and his lower jaw jutted out as if daring her to argue.

Molly saw Aunt Karen and Uncle Phil look at each other in a knowing way. She didn't say that *her* door had also been shut and Buckie scratched at it until she opened it. Buckie, with Fifi in his mouth, had trotted in, curled up on the rug beside her bed, and stayed there all night.

Glendon acted like he thought she was trying to take Buckie away from him or something. What a dope.

"You'd better hurry, Glendon, or you'll miss the school bus," Aunt Karen said.

Molly spent the day watching the llamas and playing

hide-the-doll with Buckie. Buckie's strong sense of smell amazed her. He even found Fifi when Molly climbed partway up the mountain and buried the doll in a snow-bank.

When Glendon got home from school, he went straight to his room and shut the door. Molly tried not to show how disappointed she was. Was he going to ignore her for a whole month? She had hoped they would go for a hike or play cards or something. She wanted to show him how Buckie could find Fifi.

Instead, she read part of the book about llamas that Uncle Phil loaned her. When she grew tired of reading, she knocked on the door of Glendon's room.

"Would you like to play a game?" she asked, when he opened the door.

"I don't care much for games."

"What do you like to do after school?"

"Usually I experiment with my chemistry set or work on my models."

"Could I see your models?" Molly asked.

Just then Aunt Karen came up the stairs, carrying a stack of clean towels. "Good idea," she said, as she went past. "Show Molly the ship you're building."

Reluctantly, Glendon let her into his bedroom. One whole wall was covered with shelves on which sat a variety of model cars, trains, and ships. There were even some models of dinosaurs.

"Did you make all of these?" Molly said. Glendon nodded. "How long does it take to make one?" she asked.

"It depends on the kit," Glendon said.

A nearly completed model ship sat on a card table. The ship looked like it contained hundreds of tiny plastic parts.

"How do you know which piece goes where?" Molly asked.

Glendon pointed to a printed sheet of directions. "I follow the instructions," he said. "Haven't you ever made anything?"

"I make collages out of cloth," Molly said. "I've never made a model, like these. It looks like fun."

While she was looking at the model ship on the card table, Buckie trotted into the room, carrying Fifi in his mouth. Wagging his tail, he dropped the doll at Molly's feet.

"What does Buckie have?" Glendon asked as he peered at Fifi.

"It's a rag doll that I made."

"Buckie shouldn't play with that," Glendon said.

"Why not?"

"He might bite the buttons off. He might choke."

"He doesn't chew on the doll. I hide it and he finds it."

Glendon glared at her. "Buckie's my dog," he said, "and I don't want him playing with the doll."

"He won't choke. Honest! Watch, I'll show you what we do."

Molly bent over, reaching for Fifi. She suspected that Glendon wasn't worried about the buttons at all. He was just being quarrelsome. But if it would make him feel better, she'd cut the buttons off.

As Molly's hand touched Fifi, Glendon suddenly reached down and tried to snatch the doll away from her.

Quickly, Molly grabbed Fifi and held the doll behind her back.

"Give me that," Glendon said.

"No. Fifi's mine. I made her."

"Well, Buckie's my dog and I say he can't play with your stupid doll."

Buckie, apparently thinking this was a new version of the game, rushed behind Molly and lunged at Fifi. His front paws hit Molly in the back and Molly lurched forward, lost her balance, and collided with the card table.

The model ship crashed to the floor. Molly looked in dismay at the tiny, smashed pieces.

"I'm sorry," she said. "I didn't mean to break your ship."

Glendon knelt beside the broken model.

"Can you fix it?" Molly asked.

He shook his head.

"I'm sorry," Molly said again.

"You and your dumb doll."

"It was an accident. I didn't know Buckie would jump on me."

"Get out," he said. "Get out of my room."

Molly walked to the door. Buckie trotted beside her, still looking eagerly at Fifi.

What a mess, Molly thought. She hadn't meant to break his ship but it was his own fault. If he hadn't tried to take Fifi away from her, the accident wouldn't have happened.

"Buckie!" Glendon said. "Sit!"

Buckie sat. As soon as Molly was out in the hall, Glendon slammed the door. Molly was quite sure she'd never be invited to his room again.

Three

Buckie howled in the night. It was a loud, mournful howl, unlike any noise Molly had heard before. She shivered and pulled the blanket up tight under her chin.

Buckie howled again. The primitive sound seemed weighted with sadness and, from somewhere across the fields, she heard the answering howls of a pack of coyotes.

Molly opened her eyes and saw that lights were on. Buckie must be sick. Maybe he ate something he shouldn't have eaten; it sounded like he had a terrible stomachache. She wondered how far it was to the nearest veterinarian and whether he could be reached at night.

"Ooowuuahhh," wailed Buckie. The sound came from the other end of the hall, from Aunt Karen and Uncle Phil's bedroom.

Molly got out of bed, put on her bathrobe, and went down the hall to see what was happening.

Buckie sat on the floor beside Aunt Karen's bed, with his head resting on the quilt. As Molly approached, he turned and gazed mournfully at her. His tail did not wag.

Uncle Phil was talking on the telephone. "The road isn't on the highway map," he said. "It's only on the National Forest map."

She realized he was giving someone directions, telling them how to find the ranch.

"Hurry," he said, just before he hung up. "She needs help, fast."

Molly stopped at the bedroom door. "What's wrong?" she asked.

"It's your Aunt Karen," Uncle Phil said. "I can't wake her. She—she seems to be in a coma."

Buckie put his muzzle in the air and howled again. The sound sent chills down Molly's back.

"Is there anything I can do?" she asked.

"Yes. Get dressed and take the big flashlight that's by the front door. Go down to the end of the lane and open the gate. An ambulance from town is coming out and you can watch for it so they find us faster."

Molly turned and hurried toward her room.

"Take Buckie with you," Uncle Phil called.

Molly dressed quickly in jeans and sweat shirt. A coma! People in comas didn't move, didn't speak.

"Come on, Buckie," she called. "Let's go, boy."

Buckie didn't come. Molly ran back to the bedroom. "Here, Buckie. Come on, boy."

Buckie leaned closer to the bed.

"Go, Buckie," Uncle Phil said, and he pointed toward the stairs. "Go with Molly." Uncle Phil's voice sounded scratchy, as if he had eaten too many crackers and needed a drink of water.

Buckie stood up, looked once more at Aunt Karen, and trotted toward Molly. She found the flashlight on a table by the front door and clicked it on.

Beaming the flashlight ahead of her, she ran down the lane. Her heart thumped in her chest. A coma! How could Aunt Karen be in a coma? When Molly went to bed, Aunt Karen was sitting in the blue chair, knitting a sweater. That was only a few hours ago. How could she possibly be in a coma?

Molly got a crick in her side from running but she didn't slow down. She wanted to be sure she got to the gate before the ambulance came. Buckie raced ahead and then stopped and looked back, waiting for her to catch up to him.

When they reached the end of the lane, the gate was already open. The metal rod which kept it propped open was in place.

How odd, Molly thought. Who would forget to close the gate? Quickly, she shined her light across the pasture, relieved to see that the llamas were all at the far side. If they had been near the lane, they might have escaped.

She stood beside the mailbox and watched the road that led to town. Buckie paced nervously, sniffing the road, the gate, and the weeds.

Molly wondered what was wrong with Aunt Karen. She'd complained of a stuffy nose and sore throat at dinnertime but those were just the symptoms of a minor head cold. A head cold was one thing—not waking up was something else.

Molly thought a coma sometimes happened to people who were severely injured in an accident or who had a stroke or maybe a brain tumor. No one ever went into a coma from a head cold; she was pretty sure of that.

Molly walked impatiently back and forth across the road. She had to move; she couldn't just stand there. How far did the ambulance have to come? There were advantages, Molly decided, to living in the city.

Wailing sirens were a constant annoyance at home, especially in the summertime, when she left her window open at night. Fire engines and ambulances screamed by regularly, breaking into her sleep.

But those same sirens represented help in an emergency. If Aunt Karen lived in the city, an ambulance would already be here and she'd be on her way to the hospital.

A glimmer of light behind her caught her attention and Molly swiveled around to look back toward the barn. She could just make out the dark outline of the barn against the sky and she peered toward it, wondering if perhaps she'd glimpsed a shooting star.

No, there it was again, a brief arc of light, visible through the barn window. Someone was inside the barn with a flashlight. Was the baby llama being born? But who would be out there? She knew Uncle Phil was in the house with Aunt Karen. Maybe it's Glendon, she decided. Maybe he went out to check on the mother llama.

She turned back to the road and peered once more in the direction of town.

Lights ahead! Headlights and rotating red lights. Molly waved the flashlight over her head, and the headlights speeded up. She aimed her light down the lane, moving it back and forth the way she'd seen traffic cops do, to indicate where the ambulance should go.

It sped past her down the lane, the revolving lights casting an eerie red glow across the pasture. Just as Molly started to follow it to the house, the siren came on. It pierced the quiet night air and echoed off the mountainside before it faded away. Somewhere in the distance, a lone coyote answered it.

"Here, Buckie!" Molly called. She was sure Buckie knew his way home but she thought the siren might have startled him. He was already acting so strangely, howling that odd yowl and not wanting to go outside with her until Uncle Phil made him go.

After checking to be sure the llamas were still on the far side of the pasture, she left the gate open so the ambulance could get out quickly.

"Come, Buckie," she called again. She didn't want Buckie wandering away down the road. She didn't see him but she could hear his dog tags jingling in the darkness behind her.

The ambulance jerked to a stop in front of the house; two people in white uniforms jumped out and raced inside. Molly hurried down the lane after them.

She went past the white ambulance, with its red lights still going around and around, and into the house. She could hear voices, but she decided against going upstairs to see what was happening. She knew it would be best to stay out of the way.

Buckie scratched at the door and Molly let him in. He trotted past her, and went straight up the stairs. He's worried about her, too, Molly thought. He's going to see if she's OK.

Molly followed. She didn't want him bothering the medics.

"Buckie. Sit," she said, when she reached the top.

Buckie sat down near the door to Uncle Phil and Aunt

Karen's bedroom. While Molly watched, he threw back his head and howled once more.

"Ooowuuooah!"

Glendon stood in the doorway of his room, watching silently.

One of the medics was talking on a cordless phone. "Before she slipped into the coma," he said, "her respiration was slow and gasping. She's asthmatic but has never had a severe attack. We're starting out with her now; tell Emergency to watch for us."

He hung up and he and his partner lifted Aunt Karen onto a stretcher. She was wrapped in a blanket and her face was the color of fireplace ashes. They hurried past Molly and down the stairs. Uncle Phil was right behind them; Glendon and Molly followed.

"We're taking her to the hospital," Uncle Phil said, as he walked. "Glendon and Molly, you will have to stay here by yourselves. I'll call you as soon as I know anything."

Buckie trotted at Uncle Phil's heels, whining.

"Keep Buckie inside until you close the gate," Uncle Phil said. "I don't want him running after the ambulance." Molly clutched Buckie's harness while Uncle Phil held the front door open. While the medics slid the stretcher into the back of the ambulance, Uncle Phil ran to his car, started it, and pulled up behind them.

One of the medics got in back with Aunt Karen; the other medic started the engine and the ambulance roared away, with Uncle Phil right behind it. Molly, Glendon, and Buckie stood in the doorway and stared after them until the red taillights disappeared in the distance.

Molly held tightly to Buckie, while Glendon closed the door. When she let go, Buckie scratched at the door and whined.

"I guess we'd better go close the gate," Molly said.

Glendon didn't answer. He just looked at her, the way he had when the ship fell. It didn't bother her so much this time. Glendon was weird and rude but right then Molly was too worried about Aunt Karen to try to figure out what was wrong with him. If he wanted to stand there and stare at her, let him.

Glendon walked slowly toward the stairs. When he reached them, he looked at Molly and said, "A dog howls that way when his owner dies. I read about it in a book." Without waiting for her to reply, he turned and started up the stairs to his room.

Molly watched him go, her stomach churning. Buckie pawed at the door and whined some more. "You have to stay in until the gate's closed," Molly said. Glendon apparently wasn't going to do it so she supposed she would have to go back out and close it herself.

She slipped carefully out the door, making sure that

Buckie didn't squeeze past her. It seemed darker than before and colder. Molly shivered. She wished Buckie could walk along with her.

That's silly, she told herself. You weren't scared to run down the lane and watch for the ambulance; why should you be nervous now?

She glanced at the barn; all was dark. She'd forgotten to ask Glendon if the baby llama was being born but it must not be. Glendon wouldn't go upstairs to bed if the llama needed attention.

A dark cloud covered the sliver of moon and the shadowy barn faded into the trees beyond. Molly shivered once more and then stepped resolutely off the porch and hurried down the lane.

She was halfway to the gate when she thought she heard a noise behind her. She stopped and listened for a moment but she heard nothing more. When she shone the flashlight in a wide circle, she saw only meadow grass and trees.

The sound came again—a sharp, abrupt noise, like a braying donkey with hiccups. This time she could tell it came from the barn. Merrylegs. She didn't know llamas made any sound except the happy hum, but what she heard was definitely an animal noise. Maybe the baby *was* coming.

She walked faster, wondering how long it would take

the ambulance to reach the hospital, wondering if Aunt Karen would be all right.

She reached the gate, lifted the metal rod, and began to push the gate shut. As she did, an engine started behind her. Startled, Molly turned to look back. As she squinted into the darkness, a truck with no headlights on roared down the lane. For an instant Molly stood still, paralyzed with shock. Her eyes widened in terror as the truck rushed forward out of the darkness, straight toward her.

It was almost on her before she could react. At the last second, she leaped out of the way, flinging the gate open again and twisting her ankle as she stumbled into the pasture. She fell to her knees, tearing her jeans. Pebbles flew up from the truck's tires and landed like hailstones in Molly's hair.

"Hey!" she yelled, but the driver either didn't hear her or didn't choose to stop.

She watched the truck turn off the lane and head toward town; it was nearly out of her sight when the driver finally turned on the headlights.

She was shaking with anger. She might have been killed by that stupid driver, going around with no lights on in the middle of the night.

She yanked the gate shut and started to run. All she wanted to do now was get safely back to the house.

She didn't know who had been in the barn or why they would drive away without any lights. She'd been so startled when the truck came up behind her, and so anxious to get out of the way, that she hadn't noticed who was driving. Maybe it was a veterinarian. Whoever it was, he'd better learn how to drive before he killed somebody.

By the time Molly reached the house, her breath came in short gasps and her twisted ankle throbbed.

Buckie wagged his tail happily when she came inside. She reached down to pet him and he licked her hand.

She thought about what Glendon had said. *A dog howls like that when his owner dies.* She hoped Glendon was wrong. Wearily, she locked the door and then climbed the stairs, with Buckie at her side. It would be comforting to have him sleep on the rug beside her bed for the rest of the night.

When she passed Glendon's closed bedroom door, she hesitated. The way Glendon acted, she didn't want to talk to him any more than necessary. Still, she was shaken by what had happened just now and needed to find out who was responsible. She knocked.

"Glendon?" she said. "Who was out in the barn tonight?"

Glendon didn't answer.

Four

Where was she?

Blinking, Molly struggled to wake up. It had taken her a long time to get back to sleep and now she was so groggy, it took a moment for her to recognize her surroundings.

Aunt Karen's house. She was at Aunt Karen's house only Aunt Karen was in the hospital and . . . someone was pounding on the front door.

Molly jumped out of bed, fully awake now. Last night's events all came back to her as she pulled on her blue bathrobe and slid her feet into her fuzzy yellow slippers.

Buckie was already downstairs, barking, and Glendon must be up, too, because she heard a radio playing. Molly hurried out of her room. As she started down the steps, she heard the front door open.

"Are you Glendon?" a man's voice said. "I'm Sheriff Donley. Did your dad call and tell you I was coming?"

"Yes," Glendon said. "I just talked to him."

Molly crossed the hall and saw a man in uniform, letting Buckie sniff his fingers. Through the open door she saw a white car with a gold star on the side and blue lights on the roof.

"You must be Molly," the sheriff said. "Phil said you'd be here, too." He held a card out for Molly and Glendon to see. It had his picture on it. "This is my identification," he said. "I need to come in and get some things."

"Is Aunt Karen going to be OK?" Molly asked.

"I don't know," the sheriff said. "It was still touch and go when I left the hospital." He stepped inside. "I need to collect samples of food," he said. "Any leftovers of what she ate last night."

"Is that what made her sick?" Glendon said. "Something she ate?"

"Could be."

"But we all ate the same things," Molly said. "If the food was spoiled, wouldn't all of us be sick?"

"Maybe you didn't eat exactly the same things. And maybe the food wasn't spoiled. She could have some illness that doesn't have anything to do with what she ate but we have to find out. So many crazy things happen these days; we can't assume anything."

Molly frowned. What sort of illness? What crazy things?

"You think she was poisoned, don't you?" Glendon said.

Molly's jaw dropped. Poisoned!

"It looks that way," Sheriff Donley said. "We need to test the food, to be sure."

Stunned, Molly led the way to the kitchen and opened the refrigerator.

"We had pot roast last night," she said. "And potatoes and gravy." A nice, normal dinner. Nothing weird. Certainly nothing poisonous.

"We had carrots, too," Glendon said. "And salad."

Molly removed a glass dish which contained the rest of the meat and potatoes. She didn't see any leftover carrots or salad.

"Let me look," Glendon said, and he rummaged around in the refrigerator, opening containers and closing them again.

"Here's the extra gravy," he said.

The sheriff put the food into an insulated box that he'd brought along. "What about dessert?" he asked. "Did you have any dessert last night?"

"I had cookies," Molly said.

"Me, too," Glendon said, "but Mother didn't have any."

"Are you positive?"

"She didn't feel too well, even before we ate," Molly said. "Her nose was stuffy and she said she had a headache. We thought she was getting a cold or the flu. Are you *sure* she was poisoned?"

Molly didn't mean to doubt the sheriff's word; it was just so preposterous. Who would poison Aunt Karen? And why?

"What about snacks?" the sheriff asked. "Did you eat anything later in the evening?"

"We had some popcorn," Glendon said. "But all of us ate some, not just Mother."

"We all ate the pot roast, too," Molly pointed out.

"Where do you keep the popcorn?" the sheriff asked.

Glendon opened a cupboard and removed a jar of popcorn.

The sheriff put it in the box with the pot roast and gravy containers. "I don't see how someone could poison unpopped popcorn," he said, "but I'll have it tested. I'll take along the cookies, too."

Molly didn't see how someone could poison popcorn, either, but then she didn't see how any of this could be happening. She handed the sheriff the tin of cookies.

"I *know* these aren't poison," she said. "I made them myself."

"Can you think of anything she might have eaten that the rest of you didn't have?" the sheriff asked. "Anything at all?"

Both Glendon and Molly shook their heads.

"Your dad will be calling you, or coming home, as soon as he can," the sheriff said. "Meanwhile, don't eat anything from a package that's already been opened. Do you understand?"

Molly and Glendon nodded.

After the sheriff left, Molly said, "I can't believe this! Who would want to poison Aunt Karen? And how would the poison get put in the food? There was nobody here yesterday except us."

Glendon didn't answer. Molly looked at him. He was glaring at her and the expression in his eyes made her take a quick step backwards.

"Yes," he said slowly. "Nobody else was here."

He thinks I did it, Molly realized. *He thinks I poisoned Aunt Karen.*

"Glendon," Molly said. "I would never . . ."

But Glendon wasn't listening. "Wait a minute," he said. "I just thought of something." He turned away from Molly, yanked open the door and hollered, "Hey, Sheriff! Wait! I just remembered something."

Sheriff Donley hurried back to the house. "What is it?" he asked.

Glendon spoke slowly, as if he wanted to be sure the sheriff understood. "Last night, when Mother said she felt like she was getting a cold, Dad said maybe she should take one of Molly's cod-liver-oil pills."

Molly looked at him, astonished. Was he telling the truth or was he trying to blame the poisoning on her?

"Did she take one?" the sheriff asked.

"Yes," Glendon said.

Molly's stomach did a flip-flop. "Do you think that might be what happened?" she said. "Was there poison in one of the cod-liver-oil pills?"

"Anything's possible," the sheriff said. "There have been many cases of product tampering lately."

"No one in their right mind would poison cod-liver-oil pills."

"Of course not. But people died because some nut put cyanide in painkiller capsules, so it could happen with cod-liver oil, too. Where are they?"

Molly got the bottle and handed it to the sheriff. "I take one of these every morning," she said, "and I haven't been sick."

"Maybe you were lucky," the sheriff said. He opened the bottle and looked inside. "They're soft pills; it would be possible."

Molly stared at the bottle. The gold-colored capsules were visible through the glass and she thought of all the mornings when she had routinely swallowed one of them. If one of the cod-liver-oil capsules contained poison, then it could have been her, not Aunt Karen, who almost died. Almost? They didn't know yet if Aunt Karen would get well or not.

Molly had promised her mother that she'd take a pill each day, just as she did at home. If there *was* poison in one of them and if Aunt Karen hadn't swallowed the one with poison in it, Molly would have taken it eventually. Maybe, as the sheriff said, she was lucky. But it wasn't lucky for Aunt Karen to be poisoned. It wasn't lucky, at all. It was terrible.

"Call me if you think of anything else," Sheriff Donley said. "Here's my number." He handed Glendon a business card and left.

Molly fought back tears. She wished she could go home. She wondered if she should try to call her mother. Mom had told her that the office in Los Angeles would be able to reach her in Japan, in case Molly needed to get a message to her. The office telephone number was written on a piece of paper in Molly's wallet.

"But don't call them unless it's an emergency," Mom had said. "Life or death."

Was this an emergency? Aunt Karen's condition would be considered life or death but there wasn't anything Mom could do to help, even if she were here. Aunt Karen was in a hospital; the doctors were caring for her and Uncle Phil was there.

If I called now, Molly thought, what message would I leave? I'm scared. Glendon hates me and I don't know what to do about it. Neither of those reasons could be called emergencies.

No, Molly decided, I can't bother Mom with all of this. Not yet. Probably Uncle Phil will come home soon and maybe Aunt Karen, too. If they pumped all the poison out of her stomach, she might get better fast. She might even be able to come home today.

Glendon took a fresh box of cereal out of the cupboard, opened it, and poured himself a bowl.

"What time do you leave for school?" Molly asked.

"I'm not going to school. I'm going to stay home and do Dad's chores."

That reminded Molly of the barn.

"Who was out in the barn last night?" she asked.

"Nobody."

"Somebody was. I saw a light. And later, when I went back out to shut the gate, a truck drove away."

Glendon looked at her as if she'd announced that a flying saucer had landed in the pasture. "Are you sure?" he asked.

"Yes. The truck almost ran over me because it didn't have any lights on."

"There shouldn't have been anybody in the barn last night," Glendon said.

"Maybe Uncle Phil called a veterinarian. Maybe the baby llama was born. Someone might have come before Aunt Karen got sick, while we were both asleep, and Uncle Phil just forgot to tell us."

"We never need the vet for birthings." He sounded disdainful.

"*Someone* was in the barn and whoever it was ran me off the lane in the dark."

"That doesn't make any sense. Are you sure you didn't dream it?"

Molly was sure she didn't dream it. On the other hand, he was right. It didn't make any sense.

Glendon poured milk on his cereal and started to eat. Molly didn't want any breakfast. She was too upset to be hungry. Even cold pizza wouldn't taste good today.

Glendon was the most obnoxious person she'd ever known. If she had known what he was like, she would never have come here. Mom could have hired someone—anyone—to stay in their condo so Molly wouldn't be alone. Even an unknown housekeeper from one of the agencies, like they hired when Mom had her appendix out, would be better than this cousin who barely talked to her.

"I'm going out to the barn and look," she said.

"For what?"

She didn't want to say she was looking for a clue to who was there the night before—some proof that she hadn't dreamed the whole thing. "The llama," she said. "I'm going to see if the baby was born."

She opened the barn door and stepped inside, inhaling the sweet smell of new hay. She knew where to turn on the lights because she saw Uncle Phil do it when he brought her out to introduce her to Merrylegs.

Now Molly looked around the empty barn. Was it only two days ago that they had stood in the llama pen and laughed together? So much had happened since then.

She passed the ladder that led to the hayloft, and walked slowly toward the pen where Merrylegs was kept.

As she passed the stacked firewood, the garden trac-tor, and the tools that were stored in the barn, she looked carefully around, watching for a flashlight, or a scrap of paper, or some indication that a person had been here last night. She saw nothing.

When she reached the llama pen, she stopped and stared in disbelief. Then she turned and ran out of the barn, across the field, and back to the house.

"Glendon!" she cried, as she burst inside. "Merrylegs is gone!"

"Gone!" he said. "She can't be gone."

"Come and see for yourself," Molly said. "The pen is empty."

Glendon ran to the barn, with Molly beside him, and looked at the empty llama pen. Then he turned and ran outside again.

Molly followed. "Where do you think she is?" Molly asked.

Glendon shook his head. "Dad put her in last night. I saw him do it."

"Maybe the person who drove off in the truck last night let Merrylegs out."

Glendon scowled. "I'm going to look around," he said. "Maybe she got loose somehow. Maybe Dad didn't get the door of the pen shut tightly."

"It's shut now," Molly said, "and I didn't touch it."

"If someone was here with a truck, why didn't we see the truck when the ambulance came?"

"Maybe we were too upset to notice."

"I think we'd notice a strange truck parked by our barn."

"How much are llamas worth?" Molly asked.

"Male llamas cost about a thousand dollars. Females cost several thousand."

"Several thousand dollars?" Molly was astonished. She had no idea the llamas were so valuable. And Merrylegs was going to have a baby soon, so she'd be worth even more.

"The most we ever got for one was ten thousand."

Molly said softly, "I think she was stolen. We should call the sheriff and report it."

"I'll look for her first," Glendon said. "Let's be sure she's gone before we call the sheriff." He went around the corner of the barn to the back side.

Molly knew he was being stubborn. He didn't want to admit that Merrylegs had been stolen because that would mean Molly was right about seeing a light in the barn last night and about the truck that drove away.

Molly walked slowly back to the llama pen. Someone was here last night and she needed to find something, anything, to identify that person.

At least this explained why the gate had been left open and why the truck driver didn't have any lights on in the middle of the night. He was stealing the llama; Merrylegs was in the back of the truck.

She scrutinized every foot of the llama pen but found nothing.

She decided to call the sheriff herself. If Glendon didn't have sense enough to report the theft, she would have to do it. It would probably make him angry if she called, but what difference did that make? He was already angry at her anyway.

"My cousin," she said out loud, as she gave the side of the pen a kick, "is a jerk." She heard a faint scuffling sound and whirled around. She thought Glendon had gone outside. She would never call him a jerk to his face, even if it was true.

He wasn't behind her and she realized the noise had come from overhead.

She looked up just as a huge bale of hay tumbled over the edge of the loft. It was a solid, oblong bale, bound tightly with wire, and the sight of it falling rapidly toward the top of her head made her freeze momentarily. She quickly recovered her senses and leaped backwards, trying to jump out of the way, but she couldn't move fast enough.

The heavy hay landed on her shoulder, sending a sharp pain through her arm. As she fell, she hit her head on the railing of the pen. She tried to yell but no sound came from her lips. The barn walls seemed to whirl briefly in a circle and then everything went black.

Five

Sheriff Donley drove her to the hospital.

"I'll need to talk to Phil about the missing llama," he said. "And we should have a doctor check you. I think they'll want to X-ray that shoulder."

Her shoulder throbbed. Molly tried to concentrate on what Sheriff Donley was saying but it was hard to pay attention when she hurt so much.

"That bale must have been pushed to the edge of the opening accidentally," the sheriff said. "No telling how long it's teetered there."

She winced as the sheriff's car hit another hole in the road. Even though she was lying against a pillow in the back seat, every bump they hit felt like someone was pounding on her with a hammer.

She didn't know how long she lay unconscious in Merrylegs' pen. Once she thought she saw Uncle Phil standing beside her. She struggled to open her eyes, wondering when he had shaved off his beard, but she was too woozy to talk to him.

When she finally came to, Glendon was shaking her and asking what had happened. Uncle Phil was still at the hospital, so Glendon called Sheriff Donley for help.

"Seems a bit strange that so much has gone wrong in the last day," the sheriff said. He glanced at her in his rearview mirror. His face looked grim. "It doesn't add up," he said.

"It sure doesn't."

"Just since you got here," he said.

Molly didn't answer. She didn't know what to say.

Sheriff Donley put his foot on the brake and Molly tried to brace herself with her feet, to avoid sliding off the seat.

He pulled the car to a stop and then turned in his seat and looked closely at Molly. "Why did you come here for a visit?" he asked.

"Mom had to go to Japan on business and there wasn't anyone to stay with me."

"Where's your father?" Sheriff Donley asked.

"He lives in Colorado."

"When did you last see him?"

"If you think my dad had anything to do with this," Molly said, "you're all wrong. He doesn't even know I'm here."

"Oh?"

"He got married again right after he and Mom were divorced. He has two little boys and I go there every summer for two weeks. Except for that, we don't keep in touch too much. I was going to write him a letter and tell him I'm here but I didn't do it yet."

The sheriff nodded, pulled the car back onto the road, and continued driving.

Molly closed her eyes and took a deep breath. What was the sheriff getting at? Why did he ask so many questions?

She wondered how much farther it was to the hospital. She hoped the X-rays would show that her shoulder wasn't broken.

Sheriff Donley had said she'd be lucky if that's all it was. She wished he'd quit telling her how lucky she was. First it was the cod-liver-oil pills and now . . . Molly's eyes flew open as she realized what the sheriff was thinking. He thought someone was trying to kill her!

Was he right? Molly's mouth felt dry and she stared upward at the roof of the sheriff's car. Someone had put poison in the food Aunt Karen ate—or maybe, if Glendon was telling the truth, in one of Molly's cod-liver-oil pills. Someone drove fast down the lane last night with no lights on and nearly hit her. And now a heavy bale of hay fell on her. Had it tumbled accidentally—or was it pushed? Was the poison that made Aunt Karen so sick meant for Molly? Did the truck driver intend to hit her?

Three separate incidents in less than twenty-four hours were too much to be a coincidence. Still, Molly knew no one who would want to harm her. She got along with everyone, except . . . Glendon. Molly thought about the way Glendon had looked at her that morning. An icy look, full of hatred.

She swallowed. Was it possible? Could Glendon be trying to kill her?

No. He might not like her but he was still her cousin. Even though he was angry because she broke his model ship, and jealous because Buckie liked to play with her, surely he wouldn't try to kill her. Would he?

She thought back to the truck incident. What if it *was* Glendon in the barn last night? Could it also have been Glendon who drove away in the truck? Did he know how to drive? She knew that kids in rural areas sometimes learn to drive farm equipment long before city kids ever think of getting behind the wheel of a car. Maybe Uncle Phil had taught Glendon to drive the truck so that he could help on the ranch. Maybe that's who tried to run her down last night. He knew she was walking down the lane, alone, to close the gate. Could he have run out to the truck in the dark, started it, and come after her?

Afterwards, when she knocked on his bedroom door, there was no answer. Was it because he didn't want to speak to her or because he wasn't there?

And today, when he said he was going to look for Merrylegs, is that what he really did? Or did he sneak up the ladder to the hayloft, look down at Molly, and deliberately push the hay over the edge?

A tear slid down Molly's cheek and she turned her head to let it soak into the pillow. She wondered if she should tell Sheriff Donley what she was thinking. Would he believe her? He might think she was imagining things or trying to get Glendon in trouble. She didn't know how Uncle Phil would react, either, and if she told the sheriff, he would tell Uncle Phil.

And what would Glendon do if they questioned him or accused him? He'd deny it, of course, and she had no proof. If he *didn't* know how to drive and had nothing to do with the bale of hay, how would he feel about being accused? He'd really hate her then.

Molly decided to say nothing yet. Probably there was no connection between the poisoning and the truck and the hay. Probably there was no one trying to harm her at all. And even if there was, she was safe now. They were almost to the hospital and Uncle Phil would be there and nothing could happen to her with all the nurses and doctors around.

Sheriff Donley had called, so the hospital staff was expecting her. Uncle Phil was waiting for her, too, and she was so glad to see him, she nearly cried. He had dark circles under his eyes and his clothes looked rumpled.

"What happened?" he asked, as he helped Molly out of the car.

"I was in Merrylegs' pen. She's gone and . . ."

"Gone! Gone where?"

"We don't know. When I went to the barn this morning, she wasn't there and before I could call you, the hay fell on me."

"Has the lab report come back yet?" Sheriff Donley asked.

"We just heard from them," Uncle Phil said. "All the food checked out OK. They're testing the cod-liver-oil pills now. They suspect cyanide."

Molly forgot her aching shoulder. Glendon was right. If all the food was OK, it must be the cod-liver-oil pills. Her vitamins had poison in them. She felt queasy.

"Is she going to be all right?" she whispered.

"She's still unconscious, but at least she's alive. And Karen's a fighter; I think she'll make it."

"Do you know where the pills were purchased?" Sheriff Donley asked Molly.

"I'm not positive," Molly said. "But probably at the Castle Store by our condo. That's where Mom usually shops."

"I already have a call in for your mother," Uncle Phil said.

"As soon as we know for sure that it's the pills, we'll alert all the Castle Stores in Los Angeles County," Sheriff Donley said. "If someone tampered with one bottle, they may have tampered with more. We'll need to call the manufacturer, too. This is big trouble for them."

By then, Molly had been instructed to lie down on a gurney and a nurse had strapped her on, so she wouldn't fall off. As the nurse pushed Molly out of the room, she heard Sheriff Donley still talking to Uncle Phil.

"We'll get the FBI in on it," he said. "The pills were purchased in California and the victim swallowed one in Washington. It isn't a local problem."

"I thought all bottles were sealed somehow, so they're tamperproof," Uncle Phil said.

Molly couldn't hear anymore. She was wheeled around a corner and into the X-ray room.

The X-rays were negative. "No broken bones," the doctor told Molly.

She was happy to hear it. It hurt whenever she moved but at least she didn't need a cast or a sling and she didn't have to stay in the hospital.

"The shot we gave you will take care of the pain for

several hours," the doctor said. "After that, you should be able to get by with aspirin. Call if you have any problem but I expect you'll be as good as new in a day or two."

"I'll drive Molly home," Sheriff Donley said. "Do you want me to notify anyone about your llama?"

"I'll make the calls; I can do that from here."

"You need to go home and get some sleep," the doctor said. "Let the sheriff worry about your llama."

"I must alert the other llama breeders in the state," Uncle Phil said. "If anyone tries to sell Merrylegs, I want the word out that she's mine."

Uncle Phil sounded terribly upset. Molly knew it wasn't just because Merrylegs was an expensive animal. She'd seen him singing to the llama and touching noses with it. Uncle Phil really loved Merrylegs and now he might never see her again.

"You need some rest," the doctor said. "There's nothing you can do for Karen here. We're watching her constantly and I'll call you if there's any change."

"Can you walk to the car, Molly?" Uncle Phil asked. "Or do you need a wheelchair?"

"I can walk."

"Let's go."

They drove home in silence. Molly wanted to ask how soon Uncle Phil thought Mom might call and when Aunt Karen might be well enough to come home but the shot the doctor gave her for pain made her sleepy and she couldn't quite manage to say the words. The questions tumbled hazily in her mind as her head drooped slowly toward her chest. Finally she gave in, closed her eyes, and slept.

When the car stopped and Uncle Phil got out to open the gate, Molly woke up. She felt better. Her shoulder didn't hurt much at all, the sun was shining, and soon she'd get to talk to Mom on the phone.

Glendon seemed surprised to see her. Apparently, he expected her to stay at the hospital. She suspected he was disappointed. "How's Mother?" he asked.

"Still unconscious," Uncle Phil said.

"Have they figured out what's wrong with her?" Glendon asked.

Uncle Phil sank into a chair and told Glendon everything that had happened.

While he talked, Molly fixed him a sandwich. He looked exhausted and she was quite sure he'd eaten nothing since the night before.

When Uncle Phil got to the part about the laboratory and how they were now testing the cod-liver-oil pills, Molly sensed that Glendon was staring at her again. She turned to him and he quickly looked away but not before she saw the hatred in his eyes.

She knew he already suspected her and she was sure this convinced him that she was guilty. She's the one who brought the bottle of pills here and who told Aunt Karen that they might help prevent a head cold. Whether Molly actually put the poison there or not, there was no getting around the fact that if it hadn't been for her, Aunt Karen would never have swallowed that cod-liver-oil pill.

"It could be worse," Uncle Phil said. "If Karen hadn't taken the pill, Molly would have and Molly weighs much less than Karen. If one pill made Karen this sick, it would surely have killed Molly."

Molly shivered. She looked at Glendon again. He had watched her swallow one of the pills yesterday morning. Surely he must realize that she wouldn't do that if she knew some of them contained poison. Unless . . . unless they *hadn't* contained any poison then. Everyone was assuming that the bottle of pills was tampered with before they were purchased. But maybe that wasn't true. Maybe the poison had been added later; maybe it was added yesterday, after Glendon learned that Molly took one of the pills every day.

Glendon *did* guess quickly that the sheriff suspected Aunt Karen had been poisoned. Was it because he already knew? Did he try to poison Molly? Did his plan backfire, so he accidentally poisoned Aunt Karen instead?

Her stomach felt all knotted up, the way it did when she had to give a speech in school. Was her cousin really capable of trying to poison her? Could he possibly hate her that much? And even if he did, where would he get the poison?

She knew he had a chemistry set in his room but chemistry sets don't contain lethal poisons. Then she remembered the shed. Aunt Karen and Uncle Phil had showed her the shed that first day, after they showed her the barn. It held mostly garden tools—shovels, rakes, and a pitchfork—but there was also a shelf of fertilizers and pesticides.

Molly hadn't paid close attention to them at the time. All she could remember now was a shelf of bottles and boxes but she was quite sure some of them said CAUTION on the label, and at least one of them had a Mr. Yuk symbol so it must contain some kind of poison. She decided that at the first opportunity, she'd go out to the shed and take a closer look at those bottles.

"I need to make some calls about Merrylegs," Uncle Phil said and he reached for the phone.

Glendon went outside and Molly decided to follow him.

"Do you think there's a chance you'll get Merrylegs back?" she asked.

Glendon shrugged. "It depends on where the thief takes her."

They walked along in silence for a moment while Molly thought back over everything that had happened. She wasn't sure if she should be trying to convince Glendon that she would never purposefully do anything to hurt Aunt Karen, or if she should be trying to find out whether Glendon was trying to hurt her.

"This morning you said you were going to do your Dad's chores," she said. "What did you have to do?"

"I just took some hay to the llamas in the upper pasture."

"How do you get the hay up there?"

"We have a truck."

Molly's heart beat a little faster. "Do you know how to drive it?" she asked.

"Sure."

"In California, you can't get a driver's license until you're sixteen."

"I can't get a license here, either, but I've been driving since I was ten. Not on the road, not where any other cars would be. I only take food to the pasture."

"What kind of truck is it?"

"A pickup. With four-wheel drive."

"Where do you keep it? I didn't see any truck."

"It's parked out behind the barn, where we load the hay on it."

"Do you have your own keys? Can you drive it any time you want to?"

"We always leave the keys in it. Usually I'm only allowed to drive when Dad's with me but today I had to do it alone." He looked at her suspiciously. "Why are you so interested in the truck, anyway?"

"No reason. I was just curious because I don't know how to drive and I don't know anyone else our age who can drive."

Glendon shrugged. "I can drive the tractor, too," he said.

He doesn't need to tell me this, Molly thought. If he was the one in the truck last night, he probably wouldn't admit now that he knows how to drive.

Her shoulder was starting to ache again and she realized the pain shot that the doctor gave her was wearing off.

"I think I'll go back inside and lie down for awhile," she said.

Glendon didn't answer her. When she turned and headed back toward the house, he kept walking.

This is my chance, she thought. When she reached the house, she looked back to make sure Glendon wasn't watching her. Then she went around the back side of the house, toward the shed.

She stood in front of the shelf and looked at the row of bottles. The first one was an insect spray. The label said DANGER and gave a list of hazards to humans and domestic animals. She read quickly: corrosive to eyes; avoid contact with skin or clothing. *Harmful if swallowed.* She turned the bottle and read the list of ingredients. It said nothing about cyanide.

The next bottle was a weed killer. It didn't contain cyanide, either.

One by one, she picked up each container and carefully read the labels. Each had various warnings; none contained cyanide.

What now? There wasn't any cyanide in the shed, so what was her next step? Should she just wait to see what happened or should she tell Uncle Phil her suspicions, even though she had no evidence?

She wished Mom would hurry and call. Molly usually felt pretty grown up and able to handle any situation but this mess was fast getting out of hand and she knew she needed advice. Mom would listen and would tell her what to do.

Molly shut the shed door behind her and returned to the house.

"Where were you?" Uncle Phil asked. "You missed the call from your mother."

"Mom called? Is she coming home?"

"No. She offered to come but I told her there isn't anything she can do for Karen. She was upset about the cod-liver-oil pills. She said she got them at the Castle Store, like you thought, only she bought them quite awhile ago. There was a sale and she stocked up."

"Did you tell her what happened to me?"

"She was worried about your shoulder but I told her that the doctor says you'll be fine and there's no reason for her to cut her trip short. She said to give you her love."

Molly bit her lip to keep from bursting into tears.

"Could we call her back, so I can talk to her?"

"No. We were lucky to get a message to her at all. She was just leaving to visit some of the smaller cities. She'll call again tomorrow."

Molly couldn't believe what she was hearing. Someone almost ran her down in the dark; someone nearly killed her with a bale of hay; her cousin hated her; the cod-liver-oil pills that she took daily contained poison—and there was no reason for Mom to cut her trip short.

"Did you tell her everything?" Molly asked. "About Merrylegs being stolen and the truck that almost hit me and . . ."

"What truck?"

Molly realized that Uncle Phil didn't know the whole story. In all the excitement about her injured shoulder, and Merrylegs, and the pills, she'd never told him. She explained exactly what had happened the night before.

"The sheriff asked me a lot of questions," she said.

"What sort of questions?"

"About my dad. About the hay falling." Molly's lip quivered as she answered. "I got the feeling he thought maybe it wasn't an accident. Maybe . . ." Molly struggled to control her tears.

Uncle Phil came to her and put his arms around her.

"Oh, Molly," he said, as he hugged her close. "Nobody's trying to hurt you. The falling hay was an accident, that's all. That bale was probably on the edge of the loft for days and you just happened to be underneath it when it finally toppled over. And the thief was driving without lights so we wouldn't see him. He didn't know you were there and he probably never saw you. As for the poisoned pills, we don't know for sure yet that they do contain poison but if they do, that's a situation where Karen was the innocent victim of a crime committed by a stranger."

He dropped his arms and bent to look directly into her eyes. "The sheriff has to consider every possible angle," he said. "That's his job. But don't let him give you any notions that someone might be trying to hurt you. Who would it be? We both know it wouldn't be your father. And all of us love you; you know that. Who could gain anything from hurting you?"

Molly hesitated. Should she tell him her suspicions? Glendon didn't love her, no matter what Uncle Phil said. But would he try to kill her? She thought of the pesticides in the shed; she'd been wrong when she thought that Glendon used one of them to poison the pills. Maybe she was also wrong to think he was the driver of the truck last night.

On the other hand, if Glendon *was* responsible, she ought to make Uncle Phil aware of it and the sooner the better. It was foolish not to tell. If Glendon tried to kill her three times, he would probably try again and Molly's luck wouldn't last forever.

Yes. Even though Glendon was Uncle Phil's son and it might be difficult for all of them, she decided she should tell.

She took a deep breath. "Uncle Phil," she said, "I don't think Glendon likes . . ."

The telephone rang. With her nerves already tense, Molly jumped.

Uncle Phil answered it. He listened, a look of horror on his face. "I'll be right there," he said.

He hung up and grabbed his jacket. "I'm going back to the hospital," he said. "Karen's worse; they think she's dying."

Before Molly could reply, he was out the door.

Slowly, she climbed the stairs to her room. She found a piece of paper and a pen and began to write:

Dear Mom:

    Someone's trying to kill me.

Six

"Glendon?" Molly cupped her hands around her mouth and yelled again. "Glen-don!"

The wind had come up and it gusted around her, whipping her hair into her eyes. Where was he?

She put her letter in the mailbox and put the mailbox flag up, looking down the road toward town. It was pointless to hike in that direction, hoping to find him, when she had no idea where he was. She turned and started back. Maybe he was in the barn.

Loneliness filled her as she looked up at the gray sky and the towering mountain. In photos, mountains always looked beautiful. This one looked menacing. It was so desolate here. There were no neighbors, no friends, not even a grocery store close enough to walk to. No wonder Glendon was odd. He'd lived here on the mountain most of his life. If she had to live here all the time, she'd probably be a little strange, too.

How did Aunt Karen stand it? Yet her letters always sounded so cheerful. She wrote about the wildflowers and the llamas—about picking huckleberries in the summer and skiing in the winter.

Molly's eyes filled with tears. Aunt Karen was dying. Right now, this very minute. Glendon didn't know it yet but he might never see his mother again.

How would he feel when he found out? For the first time since her arrival, Molly felt sorry for Glendon. She called his name again and walked faster.

Molly entered the barn and called again. There was no answer. She went in anyway, and headed for the pen where Merrylegs belonged.

As she walked quietly past the tractor, she heard something. She stopped and listened. There it was again—a muffled sound, like an animal whimpering. Was it possible that Merrylegs had come back? Could llamas find their way home, the way dogs and cats sometimes do? Maybe she hadn't been stolen, after all.

Molly tiptoed toward the pen, moving cautiously, glancing frequently at the hayloft. She didn't want any more accidents, thank you.

The pen was still empty. There was no sign of Merrylegs. Molly walked back through the barn and then, on impulse, started up the ladder to the hayloft. Partway up, she stopped. Heights bothered her and the open ladder made her feel insecure.

She pressed her legs against the rungs for a moment, to steady herself, and decided to go back down. She heard the noise again. It was louder this time and she knew instantly what it was. Someone was in the loft, crying.

Quickly, before she could change her mind, she climbed up the ladder until she could see into the loft. Glendon was huddled against a bale of hay with his back to her and his head on his arms. His shoulders shook with sobs.

Molly hesitated. Her first impulse was to scramble up into the loft and hug him and tell him she understood. That's what she would have done with any of her friends in Los Angeles.

But Glendon was different. She wasn't sure how he'd feel about having her see him cry.

Quietly, she backed down the ladder. She gripped the sides and closed her eyes, pretending each step was the last one before the floor.

When she got to the bottom, she called out, "Hey, Glendon! Are you in here?" Then she started up the ladder again. When she was partway up, she yelled, "I need to talk to you."

She climbed slowly, to give Glendon time to wipe his eyes and pull himself together. By the time she poked her head up to where she could see him, he was stretched out on the hay, pretending he was taking a nap.

He didn't open his eyes. "Can't a person sleep in peace?" he said.

"I'm sorry to wake you up but I thought you should know your dad got called back to the hospital."

His eyes flew open. "Mother? Is she . . . ?"

Looking at his stricken face, Molly couldn't bring herself to tell him that Aunt Karen was dying, that by now she might already be dead.

"She's worse."

Glendon rolled over so that his back was to her.

"I'm sorry, Glendon," Molly said.

Instantly, he turned to face her again. "You should be," he said, his voice low and full of malice. "If it wasn't for you, none of this would have happened."

"That isn't fair. I didn't know someone had put poison in the cod-liver-oil pills."

"If you hadn't come, Mother wouldn't have taken one of them. She wouldn't be so sick."

"Don't you think I know that? I feel terrible about it. I'd give anything if it had never happened. But no matter how awful it makes me feel, I still know it wasn't my fault."

"Everything was OK until you came. Now Mother's in the hospital and Merrylegs is missing and . . ."

"I suppose you're going to blame me because Merrylegs is gone, too."

"The minute you got here, it was just like before, with Mother making a big fuss over you and hugging you and telling you how wonderful you are."

"Just like before? What are you talking about? I've never been here before."

He was sitting up now, leaning toward her and, in the dim light of the hayloft, his eyes seemed to glow with a fierceness that frightened her.

"You're just like her, you know that? You even look like her."

"Like who?" Molly wanted to reach over and shake him. "I don't have any idea who you're talking about."

"You're just like Gladys." He spat the name out, as if saying it was distasteful to him.

"Gladys! Who's Gladys?"

"As soon as I saw you, that first day, I knew we were going to have trouble."

"How? How could you know any of this would happen?"

"Why don't you just go back to Los Angeles?"

"Believe me, there's nothing I'd like better."

"Good. Because as long as you're here, nothing will ever be right."

"You still haven't told me who Gladys is." She'd never

heard Mom mention anyone in the family named Gladys.

"I don't want to talk about her." Glendon closed his eyes. "If you don't mind," he said, "I'd like to finish my nap."

She could tell there was no point asking him anything else. There wasn't much use talking to Glendon, period. She didn't know why she even bothered to find him and tell him Aunt Karen was worse. She only did it because she felt sorry for him. She still felt sorry for him but that didn't mean she liked him.

"I'm going inside," she said.

As usual, Glendon didn't answer.

Molly walked slowly back to the house. She wondered how long it took an airmail letter to reach Japan.

Buckie ran across the pasture to greet her, ears flapping, tail wagging. Molly bent down and rubbed Buckie's ears. She wondered if Buckie could tell that Aunt Karen was worse, even though she was miles away. If so, would Buckie howl again?

She decided to get Fifi and play a game of find-the-doll to keep her mind off her troubles. Since Glendon was up in the hayloft, he wouldn't see Buckie with the doll and raise a fuss.

They played a few times but it wasn't as much fun as usual. Molly couldn't concentrate on the game. She kept thinking about Aunt Karen.

The house seemed too quiet. She wished she had

someone to talk to. If Aunt Karen were here, she would tell Molly who Gladys was.

But Aunt Karen wasn't here and she might never be here again.

Buckie nudged Molly's knee. Fifi was lying on the floor by Molly's feet and Buckie wagged his tail as if to say, "Hide Fifi again!"

"We'll play later," Molly said. She got out the box of dog biscuits and gave Buckie a treat. Then she put on a sweater, and opened the door. She hadn't yet climbed up the mountain to the high pasture where the other llamas were and she was curious to see them. Maybe some fresh air and exercise would make her feel better, too.

She wasn't sure if Buckie was allowed to go to the upper pasture or not so she left him in the house.

The grade was steep and she quickly reached snow level. Tire tracks in the snow made the path easy to follow.

She continued to climb, stopping once to remove her sweater and tie the sleeves around her waist. Although the air was cool, the exercise made her warm.

Soon the path grew narrow and the snow was deeper but she could still walk easily by following the tire tracks. There was a huge boulder ahead with an odd-shaped top. It looked like a gigantic arrowhead except the tip was broken off. The path turned and went around the side of the boulder.

Molly rounded the turn and stopped. A black pickup truck blocked the path ahead of her; there was a llama tied in the back of it.

Molly was so surprised that she just stood still and gaped. On the far side of the truck, a man came into view, walking slowly toward another llama. He held a rope in his hand and it was clear that he was trying to catch that llama, too, and load it in the truck.

For an instant, she thought it was Uncle Phil. She stared at him, narrowing her eyes so she could see better. The man was tall, like Uncle Phil, and had the same thick build. But this man had no beard.

Molly got a dry feeling in her throat. She swallowed hard. The man didn't see her. Maybe if she stood perfectly still until he turned away, he wouldn't know that she was there.

She was sure it must be the same man who stole Merrylegs; the one who ran Molly off the lane in the dark.

The llama moved away from him. The man swore and lunged at it. The llama began to run toward the truck. When the man followed it, Molly quickly stepped back so that she was hidden by the boulder. Had he seen her?

She waited for a second, her pulse racing. If he'd seen her, surely he would call to her. She heard nothing. As quietly as she could, she started to run back down the path.

She would call Sheriff Donley and tell him what she

had just seen. She thought his card was still in the kitchen, by the telephone. She ran faster, her feet pounding on the path.

The truck was black, with slatted wooden sides; she'd tell the sheriff that. What else could she remember about it? She should have looked at the license number. How stupid of her. What if the man drove off while she was in the house calling the sheriff? It would be a lot easier to catch him if they had the license number.

Molly passed the last of the deep snowbanks. Her side hurt and she had to slow down to a walk. She could see the barn ahead and, beyond it, the house.

Maybe she should hide in the barn until the truck went by. That way she'd be able to get a close look at the license plate. Too bad there was no telephone in the barn.

Molly hesitated. Was it more important to call Sheriff Donley right away or should she wait to call after she got the license number of the truck? She had to choose; she couldn't be in both places at the same time.

Then she remembered that Glendon was in the barn. If he was still there, he could help.

Maybe for once he would cooperate, if he understood what was happening.

She ran for the barn and flung open the door.

"Glendon?" she yelled. "Are you still in here?"

Naturally, there was no answer. Cursing her cousin

under her breath, she hurried to the ladder and started up it.

"Glendon, this is important," she said. "The man who stole Merrylegs is up in the pasture right now, trying to steal more llamas."

Apparently that got his attention because his head appeared in the opening above her.

"I saw him, up by a big boulder at the top of the path," she said. "He has a truck and there's a llama tied in it and he's trying to catch another one. Come down here and watch out the window for his truck and get the license number. Only don't let him see you." Molly was already climbing back down the ladder as she talked. "I'm going in the house and call the sheriff."

As her feet touched the floor again, a voice behind her said, "You aren't calling anybody."

Molly whirled around. The man stood just inside the barn door, watching her.

There was a gun in his hand.

Seven

"You couldn't mind your own business, could you, Miss Snoop?"

The man stood with his back to the doorway of the barn, glaring at her.

"I wasn't snooping," Molly said. "I just went for a hike. I didn't know where you were or what you were doing."

"Now you know," he said. "And maybe it's just as well. You kids can help me load the rest of those llamas."

Glendon's feet swung over the edge of the loft and he started down the ladder.

"He has a gun," Molly warned.

Glendon got to the bottom and turned to face the man. "Are *you* the one who stole Merrylegs?" he asked.

Molly looked at Glendon. Did he know this man?

"I didn't steal anything," the man said.

"Yes, you did," Molly said. "It was you out here last night with a flashlight, wasn't it? You were putting Merrylegs in your truck when the ambulance came and then you went roaring out with no lights on and almost killed me."

"Get moving," the man said, and he motioned with the gun toward the door of the barn. "We aren't here to discuss last night. I need help loading the rest of those animals and you're going to give it to me."

Molly glanced at Glendon and then started out the door.

"Move it!" the man snarled behind her and Glendon scurried out, too.

Molly headed toward the path but the man said, "Not that way. We'll take the lift; it's faster."

It was designed to be a chair lift for skiers, but all of the chairs were gone. Where two of them were supposed to be, Uncle Phil had attached a metal grill, about four feet by six feet. It was suspended by chains on each corner. How did this man know about the lift?

Molly took one look at the lift and blanched. All her life, she'd been bothered by heights. Once when Molly's fourth grade class went on a tour of an ice cream company, Molly had been unable to go with the others to the observation deck to see the ice cream put into cartons.

Partway up the open metal steps, she had to turn back and wait for her classmates down below.

Her fear of heights embarrassed and annoyed her but it was too real to be ignored. It wasn't a matter of will power; it was a matter of getting sick with fear and she was quite sure if she had to ride that lift up the mountain, she would be sick.

"You expect me to ride on that?" she said, as she stared at the cable high overhead.

The man and Glendon got on the metal grill but Molly stayed where she was.

"Couldn't I walk instead?" she asked.

The man's only reply was to motion with his head toward the lift. There was no choice. Reluctantly, Molly got on, too. The man flipped the switch and the lift lurched upward.

It was like riding on a huge swing, far above the earth. The ground quickly dropped away beneath the grill and there was nothing to hang on to for support. Afraid she might faint, Molly sat down on the grill. The metal cables creaked loudly, making her even more apprehensive.

The lift moved swiftly up the side of the mountain; the ground below them seemed farther and farther away.

Molly remembered once when she rode the Ferris wheel at the county fair and was so terrified she had to close her eyes for the entire ride. This lift was far worse than any Ferris wheel. At least the Ferris wheel went around and around, coming back toward the ground as often as it went upward. The lift went only one direction—up. She saw the tops of some fir trees far below, and she closed her eyes.

By the time they reached the llama pasture and lurched to a stop, Molly was sweating and her stomach threatened to erupt. The man and Glendon stepped off the lift and turned to look at her. She swallowed hard, trying to control her nausea, and then stood up. With shaky legs, she stepped off the lift. It felt wonderful to feel something solid, even a snowbank, under her feet again. Molly vowed never, under any circumstances, to ride that lift again. It might be perfectly safe and maybe her fear of heights was unreasonable but she could see no reason to put herself through such torture just to save a little time and effort. It would have been far easier for her to climb up the mountain on foot.

"That's Dad's truck," Glendon said when they rounded the curve past arrowhead boulder. "Who gave you permission to take our truck?"

"I don't need permission," the man said.

As they approached the parked truck, two llamas watched them curiously. Both animals stood near the back of the truck, as if they wondered why the other llama was in it. When the humans approached, the llamas moved away, staying close together and watching the people warily.

"It's Pretty Girl," Glendon said, when he saw the llama that was already tied up. "You're taking Pretty Girl."

"And that spotted one, too," the man said, pointing to the brown and white llama that he'd been trying to catch when Molly found him.

"Not Soapsy!" Glendon said. "She's my 4-H project. I'm keeping a journal about her. You can't steal Soapsy!"

"I'm not stealing anything," the man said. "I'm only taking what rightfully belongs to me."

"None of these llamas belong to you!" Glendon cried. "Not anymore."

So Glendon did know the thief. Had Uncle Phil bought some of the llamas from this man? Did Uncle Phil still owe the man money and the man was taking the llamas as a way to have his debt repaid, the way a car might be repossessed?

"You circle around the far side," the man said, completely ignoring Glendon's objections, "and herd the spotted one over in this direction." He turned to Molly. "You stay by the truck and make sure she doesn't run past it and get down the path."

Molly stood where he pointed and tried to think how they might escape. She wished she and Glendon could talk to each other alone.

Maybe we can stall, Molly thought. Maybe we should deliberately not catch the spotted llama. If it takes too long to catch the animals, Uncle Phil will come back home and discover we're missing and come looking for us. If the spotted llama came toward her, maybe she should let it go past.

Then she remembered the gun. The man had tucked it into the top of his jeans, with the handle sticking out. If she purposely let one of the llamas get past her, there was no telling what the man would do.

Mom had told her once that if she ever was faced by someone who was armed, to do what they said and not take a chance on getting killed.

Glendon skirted the llamas and disappeared from her sight.

Molly walked closer to the truck and looked inside. The keys dangled from the ignition. Too bad I'm not the one who knows how to drive, she thought. The man was on the far side of the pasture now, almost to the fence and the clump of trees that stretched upward into the deeper snow. Molly could easily jump into the truck and take off. But what about Glendon? No matter how much she disliked her cousin, she couldn't leave him behind.

Besides, she didn't know the first thing about driving a truck. Trying to do so would be foolish, no matter how tempted she was.

Molly untied her sweater and put it back on. The sun

was lower in the sky and now that she wasn't climbing, she was cold. They had better get the llamas loaded soon or it would be getting dark and she certainly didn't want to try to maneuver her way down the mountain trail in the dark.

She watched as the man approached one of the llamas. The animal looked at him suspiciously, moving a few steps backward each time the man was almost close enough to touch it. The man's jaw was clenched and his eyes were hard; he didn't try to talk to the llama or coax it to come to him.

Molly remembered how Uncle Phil had crooned to Merrylegs and how Merrylegs hummed in return. Uncle Phil even touched noses with Merrylegs when he first entered her pen and he'd explained to Molly that llamas greet each other that way. "It's an honor if a llama wants to touch noses with you," he said.

She was quite sure this man would not feel honored if one of the llamas tried to touch noses with him. For someone who apparently had once owned llamas, he didn't seem to know anything about handling the animals. Molly didn't think he liked animals much and she suspected that the llamas could sense his feelings. Maybe that's why they were so skittish with him. If he would be gentle and talk softly to them instead of trying to lasso them like a herd of wild horses, they might respond better.

The book Uncle Phil gave her said when llamas are attacked, they sometimes spit a vile-smelling green cud at their attacker. It sounded stinky and gooey. This man had better be careful or he'd have cud in his face.

She looked again at the keys to the truck. With the man on the far side of the pasture, and his attention on the spotted llama, she was certain she could get them. If she had the truck keys, then all she would need was an opportunity to slip them to Glendon.

Before the man could drive away, he would have to remove the wooden ramp that led from the ground to the bed of the truck. Maybe while he detached the ramp, she and Glendon could hop in the truck and drive off, leaving the thief behind.

It wasn't the best plan in the world, but it was the only one Molly could think of.

She edged closer to the truck, keeping one eye on the man. She stood beside the cab, on the driver's side, and slowly opened the door.

The man wasn't paying any attention to her. His eyes were focused on Soapsy, the spotted llama. Each time he got close to her, the llama moved away from him.

Molly eased the truck door open, quickly reached inside, jerked the keys out of the ignition, and shut the door again, closing it softly just until it clicked and held.

The man had his back to her, still moving toward Soapsy. Molly put the keys in her sweater pocket and immediately wondered what would happen if the man found them there. When he tried to leave and the keys were gone, he'd suspect her first. What if he searched her pockets and found the keys? What would he do to her?

She decided it would be wiser to hide the keys somewhere. That way, the man couldn't prove that she took them; he might think he dropped them himself. If she and Glendon had an opportunity to escape, she would still know where the keys were.

There was a flat rock, about the size of a dinner plate, just behind her. A scrubby bush grew beside it. Molly bent down, lifted the rock, and laid the keys underneath it. She'd know which rock to look under because of the bush.

She resumed her position near the truck, trying to look nonchalant, as if she'd just been standing there all along.

She wondered what the man intended to do with her and Glendon after they got the other llama on the truck. Surely he didn't plan to take them with him while he sold the llamas. But he couldn't very well leave them here, either, since they knew what he was doing and Glendon apparently knew who he was.

He'd already heard her say she was going to call the sheriff. He wouldn't want to let her do that, even if he had a big head start. He had to drive back toward town—the road didn't go the other direction—and he surely wouldn't want to meet the sheriff before he got to the highway.

A new thought struck her. The man did have a gun, after all. And they were in an isolated area where no people ever came. What if he chose not to take her and Glendon along and not to leave them here, where they were free to call for help, either? What if he . . .

No. It was too horrible to think about. A body hidden here on the mountainside might not be discovered for weeks. Months! Mom might never know what happened to her.

Molly wiped her sweaty palms on her jeans.

Glendon walked slowly toward the truck, talking softly to the spotted llama. "Good Soapsy," he said. "Nice Soapsy girl."

The llama stayed a step or two in front of him. She seemed to be listening but she wasn't willing to let him touch her.

Molly stood firmly in the center of the path, ready to block Soapsy, if necessary. Out of the corner of her eye, she saw the man approaching, crouching low so that the truck would keep him out of Soapsy's sight.

When Glendon had the llama almost to the ramp of the truck, the man lunged at her and slipped a rope over her head. The startled llama cried out—and Molly recognized the sound as the same kind of alarm call she'd heard coming from the barn the night before.

"You don't have to scare her like that," Glendon said. "She would have walked up the ramp by herself."

The man didn't answer. He was busy tying the rope to the slatted sides of the truck.

Molly tried to get Glendon's attention. She wanted to whisper to him to get in the truck and she'd get the keys and they'd take off alone, but Glendon's attention was firmly fixed on the man. Molly saw hatred in Glendon's eyes again but this time it was not aimed at her; it was directed at the tall man.

"I think we can get one more on this load," the man said.

"No, you can't," Glendon said.

"I'm giving the orders here, not you."

"Those other two are new arrivals. They're young and they've never been on a lead. It took us over an hour just to herd them up to this pasture. There's no way we can catch them before it gets dark."

The man looked around, as if noticing for the first time how late in the day it was. He took another length of rope out of the truck and turned to Molly and Glendon.

"Stand back to back," he said.

"You can't leave us up here," Glendon said. "We'll freeze."

Molly glared at Glendon. She wished he would quit arguing. Couldn't he see that this man was dangerous? It was better to be tied up than to be shot, and Molly had a hunch those were their only two alternatives.

The man swung Glendon around, shoving his back up against Molly's. Then he bound them tightly together, tying the rope around their ankles and again around their shoulders. Molly winced as he tightened the knot at her shoulder but she didn't cry out. It was better to be left here, she thought, than to be taken hostage. At least here on the mountain, they had a chance of survival. Uncle Phil would send out search parties; someone would find them. And they'd keep each other warm tied together this way.

She was sorry now that she'd hidden the keys. She wanted the man to drive off; she wanted him out of there, even if she and Glendon were left behind, tied up.

When he finished roping them together, the man removed the ramp, jumped in the truck and slammed the door. Then he bellowed a curse and the frightened llamas yanked at the ropes.

"Where are the keys?" he yelled.

Molly hoped she looked innocent. "What keys?"

"You know damn well what keys. The truck keys. I left them in the ignition and now they're gone."

"Maybe you put them in your pocket," Molly said, "and they fell out when you were following me down the hill."

He glared at her. "I *know* I left them in the ignition. I did it on purpose, in case I needed to get away quickly. Where are they?"

"I don't have them," Molly said. That much was the truth.

"Neither do I," said Glendon.

The man leaped out of the truck, ran to her, and quickly felt her pockets. She was very glad that she didn't have his keys in one of them. Next he felt Glendon's pockets.

"OK," the man mumbled. "OK. Maybe I did take them out myself. They must be on the ground somewhere. You kids can help me look for them."

He loosened the knots and jerked at the rope. Glendon stepped away from her, rubbing his arms. The man immediately started down the path. As soon as he was out of sight, behind arrowhead boulder, Molly grabbed Glendon.

"I know where the keys are," she whispered. "I'll get them and you can drive us out of here."

"We'll never get past him," Glendon said. "The path is too narrow."

"It's our only chance. Have you thought what might happen to us if he leaves us tied up here?"

Glendon looked at her for a moment. "All right," he said. "I'll try it."

He ran toward the truck while Molly went to the scrubby-looking bush. She bent down, lifted up the rock, and removed the keys.

As she did, the man leaped out from behind the boulder. "I'll take those," he said and he jerked the keys out of Molly's hand. "You brat! I knew I left them in the ignition." He shoved her toward the truck. "Get in," he said. "Both of you."

Glendon opened the door and got in. Molly followed, sliding across the seat to sit between Glendon and the man.

The man got in, too, and started the engine. As he shifted into reverse, Molly saw Glendon's hand move forward toward the door handle on the passenger's side. Before she could react, Glendon pulled on the handle. The door flew open and Glendon jumped out.

The man's foot stomped on the brake and Molly's head jerked backward. Her hands gripped the seat as she stared at Glendon.

He ran across the pasture, toward the grove of trees.

The man opened his door and yelled, "Get back here!" but Glendon kept running. He ducked under the fence at the far side of the pasture and headed up the mountain, into the deep snow.

The man turned off the truck and leaped out.

Now, Molly thought. Now's my chance to get away, while his attention is focused on Glendon. She slid across the truck seat to the open door on the passenger's side.

She had just put her feet on the ground when the shot rang out. She whirled around but Glendon was still running. The man had missed him.

The two young llamas galloped past Molly but she didn't look to see where they went. Her attention was riveted on Glendon.

He ran erratically, moving from side to side as well as forward. He was a fast runner and with this swerving motion, he made a difficult target. He was in deeper snow now and Molly wondered how he could run so fast when his feet sank into drifts over his ankles with every step. It would soon be worse, she knew. The mountain rose sharply from this point on and the snow just above them stood in drifts four and five feet high.

What was Glendon thinking of? He was crazy to run like that, when he knew the man had a gun.

The man shot again, and the noise reverberated from the side of the mountain.

Glendon fell face down in the snow.

Molly waited, not daring to speak or move. The gunshot echoed briefly in her ears and then she heard a sharp crack, followed by a low, deep rumbling, like distant thunder. It was an ominous sound and Molly instinctively looked at the man, wondering if he had heard it, too.

The man bolted for the truck. He jumped in, started the engine and roared away, careening dangerously as he went around arrowhead boulder. The llamas cried out and tried to keep their footing.

Molly stared after him in astonishment. He drove right past her! Surely he saw her standing there but he didn't bother to make her get in or to tie her up. She was free! All she had to do was hike back home and call the sheriff.

She turned back to Glendon and saw him scrambling to his feet. The shot must not have hit him; apparently he fell of his own accord.

The rumble quickly grew louder—much louder. The noise seemed closer than before, and she knew that it wasn't thunder. It was something worse, something far more threatening. She looked up the side of the mountain, and her breath caught in her throat.

An avalanche!

It slid toward her, oozing down over the boulders like thick whipped cream poured from a giant pitcher. She watched as the grove of fir trees, the last of the timberline, was completely buried. In less than a second, the trees disappeared and the slanted rays of the setting sun glistened off the smooth white surface where the trees had been.

An enormous slab of ice crashed to the ground beside her, jolting Molly out of her shock and into action.

"Glendon!" She screamed his name but her voice was drowned out by the deafening roar as more ice and snow cascaded toward her.

She knew now why the man didn't wait for her. He wanted to get down the mountain quickly, out of the path of the avalanche, before he was buried alive by the snow.

Molly turned and ran. She took huge strides, nearly losing her balance as she plunged toward arrowhead boulder.

Fine, powderlike snow billowed into the air around her ankles as she ran.

The noise thundered in her ears. Louder. Closer. Every muscle in Molly's body strained forward, trying to increase her speed.

Glendon screamed. The piercing cry came from behind her and was immediately swallowed by the sound of the avalanche.

Molly gulped the thin mountain air and willed herself to move faster. She looked over her shoulder as she ran. All she saw was a giant wall of ice and snow, speeding toward her. If Glendon was back there, he was already buried and Molly knew that she would soon be overcome, too.

It was like the recurring nightmare she used to have when she was little. In her dream, a huge unknown monster chased her. Although she ran with all her might, she was certain it would catch her. She could feel it coming closer, breathing on the back of her neck, grabbing at her hair. She always woke up just as the monster reached her and so she never found out what, or who, it was.

This time, the monster had a name. Avalanche. This time, she would not awaken from the nightmare.

Eight

It hit her from behind, first surrounding her ankles and covering her feet, much like an ocean wave when she walked along the beach at home. Then it rose to her knees and, a split second later, struck her with its full force.

Instead of knocking her to the ground, the snow swept under her, lifting her high into the air. She tumbled over and over, like a loose stocking circling around in a huge clothes dryer.

Instinctively she put her chin to her chest and clasped her hands on top of her head, trying to protect her face from the flying pieces of ice.

It lasted only a few seconds. Then, as suddenly as it had hit her and lifted her up, the movement of the snow stopped. Molly was completely buried.

Because her arms were around her head, there was a pocket of air in front of her face. Everything was dark and still under the snow but she could still breathe.

She tried to stay calm, knowing she must conserve what little oxygen she had. I'm buried, she thought, but I don't know how deeply I'm buried. Maybe I'm only a few inches below the surface. Maybe I can dig myself out.

But which way should she try to dig? She wasn't sure which direction was up. She had tumbled over and over so many times that she didn't know whether she'd landed feet up or head up. She didn't want to start digging in the wrong direction. A wrong guess would be a fatal mistake. She could die, today, buried alive in the snow.

For an instant, she panicked. Then she clenched her teeth and tried to remember what she knew about the law of gravity. What goes up, must come down. Water always runs down hill.

Water. That was it. Molly sucked some saliva to the inside of her lips and spit it out. It dribbled down her chin and froze into an icicle.

If she were trapped upside down, Molly knew the saliva would have run the other direction, toward her nose.

She needed to dig up, above her head. How far up?

Cautiously, she straightened her left arm and stuck it over her head. As it pushed through the snow, she lost some of her precious air pocket but when her arm was completely straight, she realized she could move her hand, bending her wrist in every direction.

She knew it wouldn't move that way in snow. Her hand was sticking up into the air.

She shoved her other arm upward and rotated both arms as hard and fast as she could. Sharp pains went through her shoulder where the bale of hay had hit her but it didn't matter; she was working the snow away from her head.

The hole above her got bigger and bigger until at last Molly's head was free. She breathed the cold air gratefully and then began rocking back and forth, while she clawed at the snow in front of her.

"Glendon?" she called. Maybe he hadn't been buried by the snow. Maybe he was looking for her and would hear her and come to help her.

He didn't answer and she was afraid to shout. She didn't want to start another avalanche. She didn't know if the man's gunshot was responsible for this avalanche or if it was just coincidence that the avalanche started when it did, but she wasn't taking any chances with a loud noise.

Her hands stung from the cold and she could no longer bend her fingers. She'd give anything, she thought, for a pair of mittens.

She scooped frantically at the snow with her bare

hands, using the same kind of motion she used in the swimming pool at home when she practiced her breaststroke.

Home. Los Angeles and Mom and her school seemed like parts of another world. She remembered laughing at Mom once when Mom used her electric hair dryer to defrost the refrigerator. Molly wished Mom would appear right now and aim a nice hot hair dryer at Molly's fingers.

With a frantic burst of effort, Molly broke free and lay on top of the snow. Blowing on her fingers to warm them, she sat up and looked around. Everything was white. And still. There was no sign of Glendon or of the two young llamas.

To her right, she saw an odd flat piece of rock. It seemed somehow familiar. She looked again and realized it was the top of arrowhead boulder. Instead of towering above her, it was now at her feet. She walked to the rock and stood on it.

She looked behind her, her eyes darting quickly across the surface of the snow. Where was Glendon?

Maybe one of his hands or his head was visible above the surface, if only she knew where to look.

She saw nothing. She looked down the hillside, wondering anxiously whether she should stay and search for Glendon or try to go for help.

Far below, she could see the ranch. Apparently, only the edge of the avalanche had hit them. It stopped short of the lower pasture. She could see the fence, the barn, the lane—everything just as it was before.

I must hurry, Molly thought. I have to find Glendon; I must get him out quickly. Even if he has a pocket of air, like I had, it won't last forever.

The vast white expanse of snow stretched behind her as far as she could see. How could she hope to find him?

Quickly, she looked again in all directions. She saw the cables that were connected to the four corners of the lift. Its location, behind a giant boulder, had partially sheltered it from the brunt of the avalanche.

The lift. She could take the lift down to the ranch and call for help.

The last thing she wanted to do was ride that lift again, especially alone, but she knew she had to do it. It was the fastest, surest way to get down. She couldn't find Glendon by herself and it would take much too long to hike back down off the mountain. She wasn't sure she could make it, anyway. Her feet, she was sure, were frozen. They felt like solid clumps of cement attached to the ends of her legs.

She rushed to the cables and, using her arm as a broom, brushed the snow off the lift bed. Then she slid her hands down the cable until she felt the control box.

She didn't know if it would still work or not but she pushed the switch, the way the man had done, and the lift lurched upward out of the snow.

Molly teetered momentarily, unable to get her balance. For one dreadful second, she thought she was going to fall off the side of the lift, back into the snow. Instead, she sat down, hard, feeling the jolt all the way up her spine.

She closed her eyes, gritted her teeth, and waited tensely for the bump that meant they'd reached the bottom.

As she rode, she wondered if she was doing the right thing. Maybe she should have stayed and searched for Glendon alone.

If Uncle Phil was home, it would be OK; he would know what to do. He would help her find Glendon. But if he wasn't home yet, Molly would have to call into town for help and she knew how long it took to get out to the ranch from town. Too much time would go by, she thought. Help would come but it would be too late to save Glendon.

When the lift reached the bottom, Molly scrambled off and ran for the house. Twice she stumbled and fell, then got up again and continued. All she could think of was Glendon, still up there on the mountain, buried in a snowdrift.

He might not be her favorite person but she couldn't let him die. Poor Uncle Phil! First Aunt Karen and now Glendon. She couldn't let it happen. She just couldn't!

Molly burst into the kitchen. "Uncle Phil!" she cried. "Uncle Phil, are you here?"

The only one there to greet her was Buckie, wagging his tail wildly and giving short, sharp barks of joy.

Molly didn't even stop to pet him. She ran straight for the kitchen telephone and grabbed the card with the sheriff's telephone number on it.

She dialed the number. The line was busy. Buckie came back to the kitchen, carrying Fifi in his mouth.

"Not now," Molly said. She ran to the coat closet, and put on a down jacket and a pair of mittens. Neither fit, but she didn't care. They were warm. She knew she couldn't go back up the mountain again without warmer clothes. She found a knit cap, too, and jammed it on her head. She wrapped a plaid scarf around her neck. She grabbed Glendon's jacket and tied the sleeves around her waist. She stuffed another knit cap in its pocket. If she found Glendon, he could wear them.

What else would she need? She tried to think but she'd had no training or experience in surviving an avalanche. There was no need for it in southern California.

A flashlight, she thought. It would be dark soon and she'd never find Glendon without some light. She found the flashlight she'd used the night before when she went down the lane to wait for the ambulance. Was it only last night? It seemed weeks ago. Months.

She returned to the kitchen and dialed again. Still busy. Buckie followed her and dropped Fifi at her feet. As Molly stepped over the doll, a tingle of excitement shot through her.

That's it, she thought. That's Glendon's best chance. She couldn't waste any more precious time trying to call. It would take the sheriff at least half an hour to get there, no matter how fast he drove, and by then Glendon could be dead.

She hung up the phone and bolted back out the door. On her way, she snatched the afghan that hung over the arm of Aunt Karen's rocking chair.

"Come on, Buckie," she yelled, and the dog ran past her, delighted to be going outside to play.

Buckie didn't want to get on the lift but Molly took hold of his harness and coaxed him until he was beside her. Then she flipped the switch again and she and Buckie started upward, flying high over the mountainside.

If Mom could see me now, Molly thought, she'd never believe it. Despite the pain in her fingers and toes, she smiled.

She knelt on the floor of the lift, clutching the afghan in one arm. The other hand gripped Buckie to be sure he didn't jump off. She didn't close her eyes this time; instead she stared down at the receding ranch. Except for the light she'd left on in the kitchen, nothing was visible.

It's getting dark too fast, Molly thought. How will I find Glendon in the dark? I couldn't even see him in daylight.

The lift reached the top and Molly jumped off and hit the switch all in one motion. She looked again around the vast white landscape and the impossibility of her task brought her nearly to tears. How much time had gone by since the avalanche buried Glendon? Ten minutes? Twenty? Even if he could breathe, how long did it take a person to freeze to death?

She untied Glendon's jacket and held it close to Buckie's nose. Buckie sniffed.

"Find Glendon," Molly said. She rubbed the jacket against Buckie's muzzle. "Find Glendon."

She let go of Buckie's harness and he began to run through the snow, leaping like a kangaroo in order to make it through the drifts.

"Find Glendon!"

She watched him run. His nose skimmed the surface of the snow. He was sniffing as he ran. Did he understand? Would he be able to smell anything through the snow even if he happened to be in the right place?

His sense of smell seemed remarkable when they

97

played the Fifi game but Fifi was only hidden behind the sofa and under the bed. Even when Molly climbed partway up the trail and buried Fifi in the snow, it was only a few inches of snow. Glendon might be several feet down.

Molly trudged back and forth, straining her eyes for a sign of Glendon, listening for any faint cry for help. Twice Buckie ran back to her and each time Molly repeated the command, "Find Glendon."

She was beginning to think her idea had failed when she heard Buckie whine.

Shining the flashlight across the snow, she saw Buckie, about fifty feet away. He wasn't running now; he walked slowly in a circle, his head down, sniffing the snow and whining.

Molly raced toward him. "Find Glendon," she called as she ran. "Good Buckie! Find Glendon!"

The dog began to dig. He burrowed his nose into the drift and pawed the snow, making it fly out behind him.

When Molly got there, she began to dig, too. The mittens helped. She was able to work without the sharp pain in her fingers that she'd had when she was digging herself out earlier. She knelt in the snow, head to head with Buckie, and the two of them dug as fast as they could.

The snow was more solid here. Once the avalanche

stopped, the snow seemed to harden, like cement. If the snow around her had been this hard, Molly would never have been able to free herself. She realized she was lucky to be alive.

Using the end of the flashlight, she chipped away at the crust. Except for her feet, she wasn't cold anymore. She was working too hard to be cold. She could feel Buckie's breath in her face and knew he was working as hard as he could, too. She wondered if he sensed the urgency of the situation or if he thought it was just another game.

The flashlight struck something that didn't give way when she hit it. Molly stopped digging and felt through the snow with her hand. Was it a rock? Could it be Glendon's head?

Buckie whined louder. Molly turned on the flashlight and aimed it at the spot that felt solid. With her other hand, she pushed the snow away from the hard object.

It was the sole of a shoe. Glendon was buried upside down.

"It's him," she cried. "You found him! Good Buckie! Good dog!"

She dug frantically for another five minutes. Buckie dug, too, but Glendon didn't help. He didn't move at all nor did he respond when she talked to him. Fear grew in Molly with every scoop of snow she removed. Was she saving Glendon's life—or digging out his body?

Nine

His eyes were closed.

Using every ounce of strength she possessed, she finally managed to get him on top of the snow. She removed her right mitten and put her hand on his throat but her fingers were so numb she couldn't tell if there was a pulse beat or not. She opened his jacket, stuck her hand inside his shirt, and let out a sigh of relief. His heart was beating; he was still alive. But how was she going to get him down to the ranch? He certainly couldn't walk and he was much too heavy for her to carry.

I have to try, Molly thought. He's unconscious; he needs a doctor.

He wasn't bleeding, but she knew that it could be dangerous to move an injured person. What if he had broken bones or some kind of internal injury?

She blew on her hands and rubbed them together, warming them enough so that she had some feeling in her fingers. Then, slowly and carefully, she felt Glendon's legs, first the right, then the left. There was no obvious problem. Next she felt his right arm. Everything there seemed OK, too. But when she put her fingers on his left arm, Glendon moaned, and Molly could tell that the lower part of the arm was at a strange angle. She was sure the arm was broken.

She knew she should put a splint on it, to keep the broken bone from moving and doing more damage. She tried to think what she could use for a splint. Earlier, she could have used a tree branch. Now the few trees on this part of the mountain had been buried by the avalanche.

She considered using the flashlight but the bulb end was so much wider than the handle that it wouldn't work well. She decided the best thing to do was to bind his arm with her plaid scarf.

She unwound the scarf from her neck, hating to lose the warmth. She positioned Glendon's arm as straight as she could and, holding it carefully in place, wound the scarf around and around it. She tucked the end of the scarf into Glendon's coat sleeve to secure it. The splint wouldn't get any awards from the Red Cross but it would help keep his arm straight. Now all she had to do was figure out a way to transport Glendon to the lift.

She decided to fashion a sled out of the afghan. She

spread the afghan out on the snow next to Glendon and started to roll him on to it. He moaned softly when she moved him and Molly prayed she was doing the right thing. What if he had a broken back or some other horrible injury that she couldn't detect? He might be paralyzed if she moved him incorrectly.

Molly hesitated. *If I don't move him,* she thought, *he's going to be dead.*

She had to take the chance. Taking a deep breath, she rolled him over until he was lying in the middle of the afghan. She took the hat out of the pocket of the extra jacket and put it on Glendon's head, pulling the edges down over his ears as far as she could. She didn't dare try to put his broken arm through the jacket sleeve, but she stuck his other arm through a sleeve and laid the jacket across his chest.

Then she wrapped the edges of the afghan around him, tucking them tightly underneath his back. She used to wrap her dolls that way, papoose-style.

She took hold of the corner of the afghan that stuck out beyond Glendon's shoes and started to pull. Planting her feet firmly in the snow, she leaned forward, tugging at the afghan. Glendon didn't move. Molly clenched her teeth and yanked as hard as she could. The afghan tore. Molly, who was straining forward with all her might, sprawled face down in the snow.

Fighting back tears, she got up and tried pulling Glendon by his feet. He moved slightly and groaned but the effort caused her shoulder to throb unbearably. Her feet sank through the crust of the snow with every step, making it even more difficult to move.

Buckie whined and leaned against her. She wished there was a way to use some of Buckie's strength but she couldn't think how to do it. Too bad she didn't have a rope or a leash. She could tie one end around Glendon's ankles and the other around Buckie and let the dog help pull. But she had no rope and no leash—and not enough energy to drag Glendon by herself.

She tried again, bending over to grasp Glendon's ankles and tugging while she stepped backwards. It went better that time; she moved him four or five feet before she had to stop and rest. After she caught her breath, she grasped Glendon's ankles again and then hesitated. Was she going in the right direction? She had been so frantic to find Glendon that she hadn't paid any attention to which way she was walking while she searched for him.

She looked around. It was completely dark now and Molly was no longer positive where the lift was.

She turned on her flashlight and moved it slowly across the surface of the snow. Ice crystals sparkled in the light, sending up flecks of pink and gold, but Molly was too scared to appreciate the beauty of the scene. The whole terrain was changed from the avalanche; nothing looked familiar.

She did not see the lift cables; she did not see the top of the big boulder. Those were the only two landmarks she was sure of and she couldn't find either one of them.

She couldn't even retrace her own tracks because she and Buckie had crisscrossed the surface of the snow too many times before Buckie caught Glendon's scent. She knew she'd be lucky to have enough strength to drag Glendon to the lift if she went in a straight line. If she zigzagged all over the mountain, she'd never make it.

I'm lost, Molly thought. I'm half frozen and Glendon's unconscious and nobody is looking for us because they don't know we're up here. Every inch of her body hurt.

She considered leaving him there, wrapped in the afghan, while she tried to find the lift alone. By herself, she could walk much faster. But she still wasn't sure which direction to go. What if she didn't find the lift? What if she only succeeded in wandering farther away? Then no rescuers would come and she and Glendon wouldn't be able to help each other stay warm and they'd probably both die of the cold.

She shouldn't have come back up here without completing the call to the sheriff. She knew that now. If his line hadn't been busy, a search party would already be looking for them. She should have waited. She should have stayed until the call went through. But Glendon might have died if she'd waited any longer. As it was, he might never recover. People get brain damage if they go too long without oxygen; she learned that in science class last year.

No, she'd been right to rush back with Buckie and dig Glendon out of the snow. They might be lost and cold and Glendon was still unconscious but at least he was alive.

She wondered where the man was. Did he make it down the mountain ahead of the avalanche or was he, along with the truck and the llamas in it, buried somewhere beneath the snow?

She felt sorry for the llamas but she couldn't help them now. She could only hope to save herself and Glendon.

Since she couldn't find her way back to the lift in the dark, she decided to wait until morning. By morning, search parties would surely be looking for them—and if not, at least she'd be able to see and could find the lift and get down and go for help.

She knew she should keep moving. If she could keep walking, keep her body moving, she wouldn't freeze to death. She'd seen a movie on television once where the hero made himself keep walking, even with a sprained ankle.

But what about Glendon? He couldn't move. She couldn't walk around all night, keeping warm, while she let Glendon lie there in a snowbank and freeze to death.

She pushed Glendon over until he lay on only half the afghan.

"Here, Buckie," she said.

Buckie was there instantly. Molly lay down on the afghan beside Glendon, getting as close to him as she could. Then she patted Glendon's chest. "Down, Buckie," she said. "Down here."

Buckie leaned over and sniffed Glendon. Molly reached out and stroked Buckie on the back. Particles of ice clung to his fur and she wondered if he would really provide some insulation and warmth or if the dog was just as cold as she was.

"Come on, boy," Molly said, and she patted Glendon's chest again.

Gingerly, Buckie eased himself forward and lay down, with his back legs on Glendon and his front paws and head on Molly. Molly pulled the side of the afghan up over her shoulder.

"Good dog," she said. "Good Buckie."

Buckie laid his muzzle on Molly's shoulder and licked her cheek. His tongue felt warm and Molly put her arm up across Buckie and hugged him.

If we get out of this mess alive, Molly thought, Buckie deserves a whole box of dog biscuits. Maybe even a T-bone steak.

She couldn't stop shivering but by huddling close to Glendon and Buckie, she was able to keep her teeth from chattering.

She closed her eyes and wondered if Aunt Karen was

still alive. Maybe by now Uncle Phil had called Mom again. If he had, surely she would come home this time. She wouldn't stay in Japan now, not when Molly was lost in an avalanche. Of course, she reminded herself, nobody knew about the avalanche yet.

Molly's head hurt and she couldn't think clearly. She was thirsty, too, and hungry. Maybe she had a headache because she hadn't eaten anything all day.

She wished she'd brought some food with her. She'd trade her next five year's allowance for a steaming cup of hot chocolate. With whipped cream on it. And a sprinkling of nutmeg. In fact, she'd even eat a plate full of peas or lima beans or beets. She tried to think of the worst food in the whole world. Cauliflower. Yes. Right now, she was so hungry, she'd even eat cauliflower!

She scooped up some snow and put it in her mouth, feeling it melt quickly on her tongue. I might freeze to death, she thought, but at least I won't die of thirst. It was no consolation.

She wondered if Glendon would still hate her. If they were rescued, there was no doubt she'd saved his life. Would he appreciate it or would he be just as mean as before? She wondered why he was so unhappy. She knew it wasn't just her visit that was bothering him. Something had happened to Glendon that made him so resentful. But what?

She didn't think it was because his parents were divorced. Her own parents were divorced and she wasn't mad at the world. And Glendon was fortunate that Uncle Phil had remarried. Even though Aunt Karen wasn't Glendon's birth mother, Molly knew she loved him—and he loved Aunt Karen, too, or he wouldn't have been crying in the hayloft.

If they were rescued, she planned to ask a lot of questions. *If they were rescued.* It was, she knew, a very big IF.

She dozed, woke, and dozed again. The second time she awoke, she felt something wet on her face. Her eyes flew open; it was snowing. She sat up, leaning on one elbow. A light dusting of snow covered their clothing.

Buckie's head was up; he sniffed the air and watched the snowflakes drift down.

Molly took off her mitten and put her hand on Glendon's throat. She felt a pulse.

She looked around. Despite the snow, the first faint hint of daylight allowed her to see the flat top of arrowhead boulder. It was in the opposite direction from where she'd been dragging Glendon, the night before. If she had kept going, she would never have found the lift.

She would find it now. The lift, she knew, was just on the other side of the boulder.

She stood up, her bones creaking with the effort. Every muscle in her body ached but still she felt elated. We made it, she thought. We stayed alive through the night and now I can see to find our way back.

Buckie got to his feet and shook himself thoroughly. Molly pulled the afghan close around Glendon. Without her and Buckie next to him, Glendon would get cold quickly.

As she wrapped the afghan around him, he opened his eyes.

"Where are we?" he asked.

Relief washed over Molly. "Are you OK?" she said. "You've been unconscious since yesterday afternoon."

"What happened? All I remember is a loud noise and I covered my head with my arms and then all this snow came down on me."

"The man tried to shoot you and then there was an avalanche. We've been here on the mountain all night. Can you walk?"

Glendon started to sit up and then quickly fell back. "Ouch!" he said. "My arm hurts."

"I think it's broken," Molly said. "I tried to take you to the lift last night but you were too heavy. Will you be all right here if I go now, by myself, and get some help?"

"I want to go with you."

"I can't move you. You're too heavy for me."

"OK," Glendon said. "I'll wait here."

He didn't sound very enthusiastic about it and Molly didn't blame him. She would not want to stay on the mountain alone, either.

"I'll get help as fast as I can," Molly said. "You can

keep Buckie here with you. He'll help you stay warm, like he did last night."

She tucked the afghan around his legs and then she called Buckie and directed him to lie next to Glendon.

When she started walking away from them, Buckie tried to follow her and she had to send him back. "Stay!" she said firmly. "Stay with Glendon."

Buckie whined pitifully as he watched her go but he did as he was told. When Molly looked back, she saw the dog lying in the snow next to Glendon, staring after her with mournful eyes.

Molly got on the lift for what she hoped would be the last time. She flipped the switch and the lift quickly dropped to the bottom of the trail. She didn't even have to close her eyes.

As she got off the lift, a quick movement caught her attention. She turned to look. At first she couldn't tell what it was in the gray, predawn light but then it moved again and she saw that it was the two young llamas, gazing curiously at her from beside the barn. Apparently when they bolted past her, they were able to outrun the avalanche. They appeared to be uninjured.

It's a good omen, Molly decided. It means everything's going to be all right, after all.

The only light in the house was the one she'd left burning in the kitchen. Was it possible that Uncle Phil hadn't come home all night? If so, it must mean that

Aunt Karen was still clinging to life and he didn't want to leave her. That, too, seemed a good omen.

He was probably worried though, and wondering why she and Glendon didn't answer the telephone.

She decided she would call the hospital first. She'd ask them to send an ambulance for Glendon and then she'd ask to speak to Uncle Phil. She would tell him that Glendon knew the man who stole Merrylegs. She wondered if Merrylegs' baby was born yet.

As she passed the barn and started toward the house, headlights came down the road, paused while the gate was opened, and continued down the lane. Relief brought tears to Molly's eyes. Thank goodness! Uncle Phil was home at last. Help was here.

She waved happily at the approaching headlights and walked toward them. They were so bright, shining directly at her, that she could see nothing beyond them. She didn't mind. She was just glad to have Uncle Phil here; she was glad to let someone else be responsible for getting Glendon off the mountain. She was so tired. All she wanted to do was take a hot bath, have a hot drink, and go to bed.

She was only a few feet from the headlights when the headlights went out and the engine stopped. Molly blinked, still seeing bright globes of light before her eyes. Then her eyes focused properly and a chill went through her as she realized her mistake.

It wasn't Uncle Phil's car. It was the black pickup truck with slatted wooden sides.

Molly turned and ran toward the house. If she could get to the house first, she could lock all the doors and call the sheriff. If only she had run to the house when she first saw the headlights, instead of going out to meet them.

She had not yet reached the front door when a hand clamped down on her shoulder.

"What's your hurry?" the man said.

Ten

"What do you want?" she said. "Why did you come back?"

"I had to come," he said. "I realized one of you kids might survive and I came back to be sure. Looks like it's a good thing I did."

Molly decided to try to bluff her way out. "You'd better get out of here fast," she said. "My Uncle Phil already knows about you. I made it down the mountain last night and called him. The sheriff's looking for you and so is the State Patrol."

"Shut up!" The man shook her and the pain flashed through Molly's shoulder. "You didn't call him last night. You didn't call anyone. Look at you! You're covered with snow and you're so tired you can hardly put one foot in front of the other. You just now found your way home."

His voice sounded different. Higher. Was he drunk? Or was he so upset that he was losing control?

"I talked to the hospital less than an hour ago," he continued. "I called there last night, and again this morning, and left messages for Phil. I told them to tell him Glendon had called and everything was fine here at the ranch. I said he shouldn't worry about a thing."

It took all her will power to keep from slapping him. He was the meanest, scummiest person she'd ever known. No wonder Uncle Phil didn't come to look for them. He thought everything here was OK.

"If Uncle Phil owes you money," Molly said, "I'm sure he'll pay it. You don't have to take the llamas."

He seemed not to hear her.

"We have to get out of here," he said.

Molly swallowed. "What do you mean—we?"

"I can't leave you here, can I? And I sure can't stick around. So we'll have to leave together."

"We can't go until we get Glendon. He's still on the mountain. He was unconscious all night and I think he has a broken arm. We can't leave him up there alone. Nobody else knows he's there. He'll die!"

"Get in the truck. We have to hurry."

"Do you *want* him to die? How can you?"

"I don't want anyone to die," he said. "But I can't help him now. There isn't time."

He gave her a shove and Molly stumbled toward the truck. She climbed in and the man put the key in the ignition. Molly's mind raced, trying to think what to do. She had to stall him. She had to keep him here. If she could detain him long enough, someone might come to the ranch. She and Glendon might still be rescued. What could she talk about that would make him linger?

"Money!" she cried.

He looked at her, his eyebrows raised.

"I—I was wondering how much money you got for the llamas," Molly said.

"Big money," he said. "Too bad we lost two in the avalanche."

"We didn't lose them. They ran down the path before the snow could hit them."

She decided to appeal to his sense of greed. More llamas to sell would increase his profit enormously.

"Why did you go all the way up the mountain to steal the llamas yesterday?" she asked. "It would have been a lot easier to take some from the lower pasture, right there by the barn."

"Do you think I'm stupid? I couldn't be loading those animals on the truck in plain sight of the house and the road. Up the mountain, nobody could see me."

"Well, nobody can see you now, even in the lower pasture," she said.

The man hesitated. His hand was on the key but he didn't start the engine.

"True," he said. "There's nobody around now." He looked thoughtfully at the house.

He seemed calmer now, less anxious. Keep him talking, Molly thought. Keep him here. Stall . . .

"Did you really get a good price for Merrylegs and Soapsy and Pretty Girl?" she asked.

"Top dollar."

"Didn't the buyer wonder where you got them?"

"No questions asked. I just showed him my business card for Baldwin Llama Ranch and he wrote out the check."

What a creep, using someone else's business card to make himself seem legitimate. Uncle Phil was going to go through the ceiling when he heard about this.

Keep stalling, Molly reminded herself. Keep him here as long as possible. "You make it sound easy to sell the llamas," she said.

"It was a snap." He looked toward the pasture. Then he started the engine, and put his foot on the gas pedal. The truck lurched forward. Molly clutched at the seat to keep her balance while he made a fast U-turn and headed back past the barn. A group of curious llamas watched as he slammed on the brakes.

"Those brown ones are nice," Molly said. "They'd probably bring a good price."

She didn't have any idea whether the two brown ones she pointed out were especially nice llamas or not, but she knew that's what the man wanted.

She could tell the man was still nervous. He sat with the engine idling for a moment, looking back toward the road. If he left now, she knew he could make his escape before anyone else came.

Keep him talking, she told herself. Keep him sitting here.

"What kind of business are you in?" she asked.

The question backfired. Instead of prolonging the conversation, as Molly intended, it seemed to bring the urgency of the situation back to the man's mind. He turned off the engine and jumped out of the truck.

Molly looked morosely out the window. Ten minutes ago, she'd felt elated, certain that she'd saved Glendon's life, and that help would soon be coming. Now Glendon was still lying up there in the snow with a broken arm and probably a concussion and who knows what else, and she was being kidnapped by a man with no conscience.

He acted like a crazy man. One minute he insisted they had to leave immediately and the next minute he was willing to take time to catch more llamas.

She wondered why he needed money so desperately. Maybe he was on drugs and was frantic for money in

117

order to buy more. If that was so, her chance of survival with him seemed slim.

"Get out here and help," the man said.

He took a length of rope from the back of the truck and started toward the dark brown llama. Slowly, Molly climbed out of the truck, trying to think of a way to escape.

There was no point trying to run away. She was simply too tired. She'd never make it and the attempt would make the man angry. She looked around. She saw only the path, some bushes, and, beyond the lower pasture, the lift.

She looked at the lift. She could get to it before he could catch her. She could turn it on and ride up the mountain. But then what? There was no one up there who could help her. If the man followed her, she'd only be trapped again, and Glendon and Buckie with her. It would be better to have to go away with him than to die in the snow.

Tears rolled slowly down her cheeks. Every muscle in her body ached. There was no escape.

She wondered what he would do with her. Maybe, if she was lucky, he would only make her stay with him until he got the money for these llamas. She was glad now that she didn't know who he was. She couldn't give his name to the police, even if she escaped. Maybe he would leave her tied up somewhere while he went to Canada or Mexico and then he'd call the authorities and tell them where to find her.

And if she wasn't lucky? It didn't bother him to let Glendon freeze to death; why would he do anything to save her life?

He wouldn't. The knowledge seeped into Molly's bones as surely as the cold had and it was just as chilling. He would never let her live. Why should he? If Glendon died, which seemed sure to happen now, she was the only one who could identify the thief. Why would he let her go?

No! Every inch of her body cried out in protest. She had struggled too hard to survive the avalanche; she was too proud of the fact that she'd kept herself and Glendon alive through the long, cold night. She wouldn't give up now. She wouldn't! She'd save herself somehow. And she'd save Glendon, too.

But how? How could she hope to escape when she was so tired and sore and hungry? If only there was someone to help her. She leaned against the side of the truck and closed her eyes. There was no one nearby except Glendon and he was in worse shape than she was. She wondered how he and Buckie were doing up there. Good old Buckie.

Her eyes opened and she stood up straight. Buckie was a big, strong dog and he was fond of her. Would he be loyal enough to defend her, if necessary?

Buckie minded well, because of his obedience training. Would he attack someone, on command?

Molly remembered the gun. He didn't have it in his hand today but he wore a heavy jacket. Maybe the gun was in his pocket. Even Buckie's strength was no match for a gun and she was sure this man would shoot, if necessary.

She hesitated. She didn't want to endanger Buckie's life. But what were her choices? If she didn't take the risk, she and Glendon were goners, for sure.

Molly walked toward the man. He had not yet caught one of the llamas. Each time he got a few feet from one of them, he rushed forward with the rope, and the animal would prance away.

"It would be lots faster if you used Buckie to herd those llamas," she said.

"Who?"

"Buckie. The dog. He's trained as a sheep dog."

"Where is he?" There was an edge to his voice and she could tell he was frustrated by his inability to catch the llama.

"He's up on the mountain, with Glendon. Do you want me to go get him?"

He stopped stalking the llama and looked at her. "How did the dog get up there?" he asked. "He wasn't up there yesterday."

"I did make it down off the mountain yesterday, like

I said, only the sheriff's line was busy and I couldn't wait because Glendon was still buried in the snow. Buckie went back up with me. He's the one who found where Glendon was buried. He could smell Glendon under the snow."

"No kidding."

"He's a smart dog," Molly said. "And he knows how to work the llamas."

"All right. All right, go get him. But I warn you. You try anything funny and you'll wish you hadn't."

Molly trudged up the path, not at all sure she could make it to the lift. She had never felt so tired in her life. Tired and discouraged. She hated this mountain. She loathed the ranch and the snow and, most of all, the man with the gun. She even resented Uncle Phil for leaving her to cope with all of this alone.

Keep going, she told herself. Right now, Buckie's your only hope. Wearily, she climbed on the lift and started the motor.

As the lift rose, she looked down and was struck by the beauty of the scene. The fenceposts, wearing caps of snow, marched across the white fields. On the other side of the house, the icy limbs of the Christmas trees sparkled in the early morning sun. With a little shock of surprise, Molly realized she wasn't scared. She had ridden the lift so many times that it no longer bothered her to look down.

Something good comes of everything, her mother always said. Maybe, out of all this terror and pain, she would at least be cured of her fear of heights.

Buckie was waiting at the top, tail wagging. He must have heard the lift coming.

"Good Buckie," she said, and she rubbed his ears.

She made her way to where Glendon lay in the snow. His face was pale and his lips had a bluish color that frightened her. When she left him, it was still quite dark. Now, in the bright daylight, he looked sicker than she remembered.

Quickly, she told him what had happened and what her plan was. "I don't know if it will work," she said. "If nobody has come for you in an hour, you'd better drag yourself to the lift, get down, and somehow get to the house and call for help."

Glendon's eyes filled with tears and Molly realized he didn't think he could make it.

"Your mother's still alive," she said. "She made it and you will, too."

Glendon blinked away the tears. "Mother didn't die?"

"She didn't die and you won't, either." Molly knew she was convincing herself as well as Glendon. "We aren't going to let that rotten thief get the best of us."

"That rotten thief," Glendon said, "is my uncle."

Molly was too shocked to answer.

"If you make it and I don't," Glendon said, "tell Dad that his brother stole the llamas."

"Your own uncle tried to kill you?" Molly said.

Glendon nodded. "Uncle Craine."

"Well, your Uncle Craine isn't going to get away with it," Molly said. "But you may have to help yourself, no matter how much it hurts or how hard it is. Even when your dad gets home, he won't know to look for you up here. If I don't make it, you *must* get yourself to the lift and go down."

Glendon nodded, a look of determination in his eyes.

Molly took a deep breath and turned away from him. "Come on, Buckie," she said. "You're going with me this time."

"Molly?"

She looked back.

"Good luck," he said. "And I—I'm sorry for how I acted. You're not like Gladys, after all. You aren't a bit like Gladys."

"Thanks." She still didn't know who Gladys was but there was no time to find out now. If she didn't get back down with Buckie soon, Craine would come looking for them and when he found them, he wouldn't waste time talking.

She and Buckie rode down together. When they reached the lower pasture, she sent the lift back up to the top. That way it would be there, if Glendon needed it.

She headed down the path and saw that Craine had succeeded in getting one of the llamas on the truck. He'd roped another one, too, but he couldn't make the animal move toward the truck. It was tugging and pulling on the rope like a bucking bronco.

Could a nice man like Uncle Phil have a creep like Craine for a brother? As she looked at him, she knew it was true. He had the same build as Uncle Phil and the same brown eyes. All he lacked was the beard. And the smile.

Buckie stopped. The fur stood up in a little ridge along his back and a low, growl came from deep in his throat.

Molly put one hand on Buckie's head and stroked him. Buckie stopped growling. Molly realized that Craine was concentrating so hard on the llama he'd roped that he had not heard the lift return, nor did he realize that Molly and Buckie were now walking down the path.

"Heel," she said softly. She started walking again and Buckie stayed beside her. She kept her eyes on Craine. He still didn't notice her but the frightened llama did.

When the terrified llama saw another person approaching, it panicked and jerked harder on the rope. Craine yelled, lifted his arm, and tried to hit the llama. As his raised arm swung toward the llama's head, the frightened animal spit at him. A large green cud flew from the llama's mouth and hit Craine right in the face.

It splattered onto his chest and into his hair.

Craine jumped back, dropped the rope, and the llama ran off.

If Molly had not been trying to remain unseen, she would have cheered.

Cursing, Craine wiped his eyes on the sleeve of his jacket. Then he bent over, scooped up some dirt, and tried to clean his face with it. He removed his jacket and flung it on the ground.

Molly walked faster and Buckie stayed right beside her. She crouched down as they passed the truck. For a few yards, it would block her from Craine's view.

She counted on his anger to help her. She knew he was furious at the llama and he wasn't thinking of anything except getting rid of the terrible-smelling cud that had landed on him. If she took advantage of the situation, perhaps she could get away before he thought about her.

In a few moments, he would probably wonder where she was and be angry at her for not returning with Buckie. Would he take the time to look for her? The lift was back up at the top, so he would assume she was still up there, too.

Would he ride up the mountain again? Would he go looking for her or would he give up and leave? There was no way to outguess him. If he went up the mountain, he'd realize she wasn't there. He would find Glendon alone and there was no telling what he'd do then.

She glanced back over her shoulder. Craine was kneeling down, trying to clean the front of his jacket by rubbing it on the ground. Molly walked faster. The possibility of escape gave her new strength.

When she reached the barn, she looked ahead at the long empty path that led to the house. All Craine had to do was look this way and, if she were on the path to the house, he'd know it. He could catch her easily.

She decided not to chance it. Instead of going all the way to the house, she ducked into the barn, taking Buckie with her. From the back window of the barn, she could see the lower pasture. She could see the truck. If he went up on the lift, she would see it moving and would have time to run to the house and call for help.

If he didn't go after her—if he got in the truck instead and drove away—she could hide in the barn until he was on his way to town.

She saw him straighten and look around. The llama had disappeared into the grove of trees on the far side of the pasture. The other llamas had followed it. Craine ran to the bottom end of the lift and looked up. Molly held her breath. He turned, sprinted to the truck, started the engine, and drove away from the pasture.

Molly breathed faster. He was leaving. He was so angry that he was going to leave without her.

When she was positive the truck was headed her way, she moved back from the window. She kept her hand firmly on Buckie's harness, to make sure he didn't run out of the barn and give away their hiding place.

She heard the truck go past the barn but it didn't seem to continue down the lane toward the gate. Instead, it headed toward the house. She stood perfectly still, straining her ears.

She couldn't tell where Craine was by listening so she walked to the front of the barn and peeked out the window that faced the house.

Craine leaped out of the truck. He charged around the side of the house, toward the old shed. Why was he going back there? Surely he wouldn't be looking for her. He thought she was still up on the mountain.

She waited, every muscle so tense that she thought if she were forced to bend, she'd snap in two. Moments later, Craine returned. He went straight to the truck, got in, and took off down the lane.

She watched until he went through the gate, made the turn toward town, and vanished from her view. Then, feeling faint with relief, she left the barn and hurried to the house. She stumbled as she went up the porch steps and she realized how weak she was.

Just a little longer, she told herself. Just keep going until you've made your phone call. Then you can collapse if you want to.

She pushed open the door and went inside. She felt unreal, as if she were floating on a cloud somewhere and watching herself act out a part in a play. With effort, she made it to the kitchen and saw the sheriff's card right where she'd left it, on the counter next to the telephone.

She was almost giddy with exhaustion. The numbers on the card blurred slightly when she tried to read them. She blinked and looked again, willing the numbers to focus. When they did, she picked up the receiver and held it to her ear.

There was nothing. No dial tone. No sound at all. She clicked the receiver button up and down but even as she did it, she knew it wouldn't help.

That's why Craine had stopped the truck; that's why he went around the side of the house before he left. He had cut the telephone line. Craine had made sure he'd have plenty of time to get away.

Slowly, Molly replaced the receiver. She thought of Glendon, lying alone in the snow, injured and scared. Her whole body ached with fatigue as she sank down on the kitchen chair and wept.

Eleven

She couldn't do it.

Molly knew what she needed to do, but she simply couldn't do it. Her strength was gone. There was no way she could climb back up to the lift and go after Glendon and help him get down off the mountain. The thought of moving as far as the front door was more than she could bear.

She had told him that if nobody came for him soon, to get himself to the lift and come down. But would he do it? Could he? She remembered how sick he looked when she left him. His face was too pale and his lips looked blue. She thought about how long he'd been unconscious and about his broken arm. Was he able to crawl to the lift? If he did, could he make it from the lift to the house?

He would die up there. She knew it. No matter what she had told him to do, he was too weak to follow her instructions. Glendon would freeze to death and when Uncle Phil came home, he would have to go up the mountain and bring down his son's body.

No! Molly sat up straight and brushed the tears from her cheeks. No, she thought. I won't let it happen. I won't! I've made it this far and I'll make it the rest of the way.

She stood up and a feeling of dizziness washed over her. She grabbed the back of the chair and steadied herself. Then she took a deep breath, went to the kitchen cupboard, and removed a container of hot chocolate mix.

She filled a mug with milk, heated it in the microwave, and stirred in several heaping spoons full of the chocolate mix. Leaning against the counter, she drank quickly, feeling the hot liquid on her throat as she swallowed.

She put a slice of bread in the toaster and then dunked the toast in the hot chocolate and ate it. Immediately, she felt stronger. While she ate, she gave Buckie some dog biscuits.

As she watched him crunch the biscuits, she considered trying to send him for help. She could tie a note to his harness and tell him to go to town. She'd read stories of dogs who saved their owners by running many miles for help. Buckie was smart. Maybe he would go all the way to town and find someone to save them.

But what if Buckie didn't go to town? What if he ran the wrong way? What if he chased a rabbit or a squirrel? The nearest town was several miles away. What if nobody found the note on him? Or what if Buckie got lost and never came back? What then?

Molly sighed. She knew she couldn't stay here and hope that Buckie would bring help. Not while Glendon was lying up there in the snow. She would have to save him herself.

She wished she had a Thermos bottle, so she could take some hot chocolate up to Glendon. He needed warmth and nourishment, too. But she didn't know where a Thermos bottle was and she knew she couldn't waste time and energy hunting for one.

As she finished her hot chocolate, she tried to think what she should take with her. She wasn't sure she had the strength to make it back to Glendon at all, much less carry any supplies, but she knew she should try to figure out what she was going to do before she left.

A rope. If she had a rope, she might be able to use Buckie's strength, like she'd wanted to do the night before.

Food. She put a banana in her jacket pocket, thinking it would be easy for Glendon to eat.

A splint. Glendon needed something stronger on his arm, to hold it straight while she moved him down the mountain. She looked around. A pottery jug on top of the stove contained an assortment of cooking utensils. Molly selected a long-handled wooden spoon and then grabbed a dish towel, too. Both fit in her second jacket pocket.

She found a piece of paper and quickly wrote a note. *Dear Uncle Phil: Glendon and I are up on the mountain. There was an avalanche and he was hurt. Your brother, Craine, stole the llamas.*

She signed her name and put the note on the kitchen table. If she and Glendon didn't make it back, Uncle Phil would know where they were and what had happened.

"Come, Buckie," she said, and she and Buckie left the house together.

She went to the barn first, found a coil of rope hanging on a nail, and put it over her shoulder.

Once more, she started up the trail, her legs hurting with every step she took. Buckie stayed at her side even though she didn't tell him to heel. She wondered if he sensed how tired she was. Maybe he was trying to encourage her to keep going. Or maybe he was tired, too.

As she passed the lower pasture, she saw the llamas watching her warily. Craine's rope still dangled from the neck of the dark brown one. Remembering how that llama had spat its cud all over Craine, she smiled. If the llama hadn't done that, Craine would never have driven off without her.

"Thanks, brown llama," she called. She hoped the one Craine caught today spit on him, too. It would serve him right.

As the path got steeper, it was harder for Molly to keep going. Her back ached. Her shoulder throbbed and her feet hurt, right down to the ends of her toes. She suspected that her feet had frostbite and maybe her hands, too.

Finally, she reached the lift cables and flipped the switch. She could hear the cables creaking as the lift came back down. When it reached the bottom, she sat down on it, grateful for the chance to rest.

Without being told to, Buckie sat beside her. Molly pushed the switch again and the lift swung once more into the air and up the side of the mountain. This time, she thought, it really *will* be the last trip up.

Buckie leaped off the lift as soon as it stopped and ran straight to Glendon. Molly moved more slowly. It was even harder to walk in the snow than it had been on the trail. She kept her head down, for the wind was blowing again and small icy particles of snow stung her cheeks.

"Ooauawwooh!"

Molly's head jerked up and a shiver of apprehension made the hair on the back of her neck prickle. She looked ahead.

Buckie sat in the snow beside Glendon, with his head

thrown back and his muzzle pointed at the sky. He howled again.

Molly remembered Glendon's words. "Dogs howl like that when their owner dies."

Was Glendon dead? Had she struggled up here, only to find that she was too late?

Tears spilled from Molly's eyes and froze to her cheeks. She plodded forward until she reached Glendon.

His eyes were closed.

Crying harder, she dropped to her knees beside him and rubbed her mittens on the sides of his face.

"Wake up, Glendon!" she cried. "I'm here and I'm going to take you home. Wake up!" She was sobbing now, nearly hysterical. Without knowing what she was doing, she lifted Glendon's head and held him close, trying to warm him.

"Come, Buckie," she cried, and when the dog stood beside her, she circled his neck with one arm and drew him close to Glendon, too. Buckie began to lick Glendon's face, slurping his big tongue on Glendon's eyes and cheeks and chin.

Molly rocked back and forth, cradling Glendon's head with one arm, hugging Buckie with the other.

Glendon moaned.

Another shiver went down Molly's spine but this time it was a thrill of excitement. He was alive!

Moving quickly now, she tied the wooden spoon to

134

Glendon's left arm, using the dish towel and trying not to move him any more than necessary. Then she took the coil of rope off her shoulder and carefully tied one end around Glendon's feet, pulling the knot tight. She fastened the other end to Buckie's harness.

Bending down, she put one hand firmly under each of Glendon's arms, and lifted until his head rested against her stomach.

"Go, Buckie. Go."

Buckie started forward. The rope went taut and Glendon groaned again as Buckie struggled to move. Molly lifted Glendon's shoulders higher, trying to take more of the weight herself. His arms dangled down, with his fingers trailing in the snow. She looked at the left arm. It seemed straight; the spoon was doing its job.

Slowly, slowly, they moved toward the lift. The crust of ice which had formed on the snow overnight helped. Molly was glad that Glendon wasn't any bigger than he was. She could tell it was taking every bit of Buckie's strength to pull that rope.

Buckie put his nose down, clearly straining with every step. Molly followed, trying to keep Glendon's head up, trying to help carry some of the weight.

"Go, Buckie. Good dog!"

When they got to the lift, Buckie stopped and Molly gently rolled Glendon on to the lift bed. Buckie sat beside them, his sides heaving, and his tongue hanging out.

"Good dog," Molly said, and she nuzzled her face in the fur on Buckie's neck. "Fine, fine dog."

When the lift lurched to a stop at the bottom, Glendon opened his eyes. "Molly?" he whispered. "Is that you?"

"We're almost home," she said. "Just a little longer."

She wasn't sure if she was trying to encourage Glendon or Buckie or herself but she liked hearing herself talk.

"I can see the barn now, and the house," she said. "Soon we'll have something hot to eat and warm blankets on us."

One step, two steps, three steps. Molly's vision blurred again and she began counting the steps out loud, trying to keep herself coherent. One step, two steps, walk, walk, walk, walk.

They passed the barn and headed for the house. At last, when she thought she could go no further, they reached the back porch. Buckie stopped at the bottom of the porch steps and looked at Molly. She imagined he was asking if she really expected him to pull Glendon up those stairs.

There were only two steps but there might as well have been fifty. Molly knew that neither she nor Buckie had enough strength left to get Glendon into the house. But she couldn't leave him outside. Although it was warmer down here than it was up on the mountain, it was still chilly and the ground was damp. Glendon needed to be where it was dry and warm.

She put Glendon's head down on the ground and untied the rope. As she climbed the porch steps, she swayed slightly and had to grasp the railing in order to keep from falling.

Once inside, she heated another mug of milk and stirred hot chocolate mix into it. She took a few sips herself and then carried it outside.

She sat on the bottom step, and lifted Glendon's head. He shifted and opened his eyes.

"Drink this," she said, and she put the mug to his lips.

Glendon took a sip, choked, and spit most of the hot chocolate out.

"Try again," Molly said. "You have to drink it. It'll give you enough strength to go inside, where it's warm."

Glendon took another sip and this time it went down. He took another sip and then another. When he paused, Molly took a turn. She didn't care if they shared the same mug. It tasted wonderful.

She offered the mug to Glendon again and this time he took it in his right hand and held it himself.

When it was empty, Molly said, "You need to get inside. See if you can make it up the steps."

She held out her hand to him. He took it but she was unable to pull him to his feet. She dropped his hand.

"Crawl," she said.

Using his good arm, Glendon crawled slowly up the steps and into the kitchen. Molly held the door for him and Buckie ran forward every few feet to sniff Glendon's face and lick him on the cheek.

When he was inside, Glendon put his head down on the floor.

"I can't go any farther," he said. He was shaking so hard he could hardly speak.

"You don't need to," Molly said, as she closed the door. She knew there were plenty of blankets upstairs on the beds, but she didn't have the energy to climb the stairs and get them. She picked up the throw rug from the kitchen floor and put it on top of him.

"Up on the mountain, when I came to," Glendon said, "you were crying."

"You were so still, and Buckie sat beside you and howled. It scared me. I remembered what you said and I thought . . ." Her voice quavered.

"I guess I was wrong about the howling. Maybe dogs do that when they sense death is near."

"Well, I hope he never does it again."

"Me, too." Glendon smiled at Molly. "I'm hungry," he said.

"So am I," Molly said, "but I'm too tired to do anything about it." Then she remembered the banana. She reached in her pocket, took out the banana, peeled it, and broke it in half.

"Here," she said, as she handed one-half to Glendon. "Here's your dinner. Or is it breakfast?"

Glendon smiled at her again and ate the banana. "Thanks," he said.

Molly sat at the table and looked down at her cousin. She didn't know which amazed her more—the fact that the two of them were still alive or the fact that Glendon kept smiling at her. She wondered if they could possibly be friends, after all.

She also wondered why he'd been so mean to her before.

Twelve

"Who's Gladys?" she asked.

The smile disappeared from Glendon's face and he closed his eyes. "My sister," he said. His voice was so soft that Molly had to strain to hear his words. "My twin sister."

He was silent for such a long time that Molly thought he'd fallen asleep. Her own eyelids were growing heavy and every muscle in her body ached with fatigue. She put her arm on the table and rested her head on her arm. She was so tired, so terribly tired.

"Mommy always liked Gladys best," Glendon said. Molly looked at him. He was lying perfectly still, his eyes squeezed tightly shut, as if to keep out the painful memories.

"No matter what I did," he went on, "I was never as

good as Gladys. Mommy fussed over her, and played with her, and made her little dolls. She would never make one for me, because I'm a boy. Dad used to argue with Mommy about it and that made it worse. Gladys would tease me and make me mad and then when I'd fight with her, she'd run and tattle to Mommy and I'd get punished. It was always like that—always!"

"Where is she now?" Molly asked. "What happened to her?"

"Mommy and Gladys left, when I was four. Dad says the divorce was because he and Mommy didn't love each other any more but the real reason was because Mommy didn't love me and she couldn't stand to live with me any longer. She never loved me. Not ever. She told me so herself."

"She did?" Molly was stunned. No matter what kind of trouble she got in at home, she couldn't imagine Mom ever saying anything like that to her. Even last year, when Molly almost flunked American History because she lost her semester notebook, Mom never said she didn't love her.

"She said I was a horrid, nasty boy. She took Gladys and moved to Arizona but she wouldn't take me. And I never hear from her, not even on my birthday."

Molly sat up and put her hands on her hips indignantly. "It doesn't sound like she was much of a mother," she said. "Frankly, I think you're better off with Aunt Karen."

Glendon opened his eyes and gazed up at Molly. "Yes," he said softly. "She's really my mother now, and I'm glad she is. But she might die. I might lose her, too." He looked terrified. Alone and sick and terrified.

Molly felt sorrier for him than she'd ever felt for anybody in her life. She wondered if she really looked like Gladys. She hoped not. Maybe Glendon had just said that because he was angry.

Since he was being so talkative, she wondered if he'd tell the truth about all the other mysterious things that had happened since she arrived.

"Did you push the hay on me?" she asked.

Glendon frowned, as if he wasn't sure he'd heard her right.

"No," he said. "Why would I do that?"

"What about the cod-liver-oil pills? Did you poison them?"

"Me? You think *I* poisoned my mother?"

"I know you wouldn't poison your mother but I thought you might have tried to poison me. You seemed to hate me so much and then all of these terrible things started happening. For awhile, I even thought maybe you were driving the truck that night, and tried to hit me on purpose. Now I know it was Craine, but for awhile, I wasn't sure."

Glendon looked shocked. "I didn't do any of it. Honest, Molly! I was really mad that you came to visit, especially when Mother started fussing over you just the way Mommy used to do with Gladys. It brought back all those bad times and I felt as if they were happening all over again. You even said we looked like twins and Mother said she's always wanted a daughter. But I would never poison anybody."

Molly believed him. She didn't have answers to a lot of her questions, but she believed Glendon. After all she'd gone through to keep him from freezing to death, she was glad he wasn't the one who had nearly killed her.

"Craine must have pushed the hay on me," she said. "In the barn, before I woke up, I thought I saw Uncle Phil, only he didn't have a beard and I couldn't get my eyes focused enough to realize I wasn't dreaming. Maybe Craine was there all along, up in the loft, and we didn't know it. But why would he push the hay on me? He didn't even know who I was."

"Probably he thought you were me," Glendon said.

"Why would he want to hurt you? He's your uncle. Yet he's stealing from your dad and he didn't care if you died in the avalanche. What happened in the past, between your family and Craine?"

"Uncle Craine lived with us for six months after Mommy and Gladys left. He and Dad were partners; they started the llama business together. Then one day a man from the bank called Dad and told him that Uncle Craine was cheating him. He was taking part of the money for himself instead of sharing everything fifty-fifty, like they had agreed."

"So Uncle Phil had him arrested?"

"No. They had a big fight about it and Dad said Uncle Craine should leave and not come back."

"Did he ever come back, until now?"

"He couldn't. He was in prison. Uncle Craine worked at a hardware store before he and Dad became partners. The owners of the hardware store found out that Uncle Craine stole money from them, too. They're the ones who had him arrested. He was released a month or two ago."

"I wonder why he came back."

"To steal some llamas, probably. He's been in trouble all his life, even when he was a kid. My grandma thinks he's into drugs but there's no proof. Dad's the only one who could ever get along with him but that's because Dad always sees the good in everybody. He kept giving Uncle Craine another chance. He always *wants* to think Uncle Craine has reformed."

"It must have been awful to have him live with you."

"I hated it. He was mean. He was even mean to the animals when he thought Dad wasn't looking."

Glendon yawned. Molly yawned, too.

"Let's get some sleep," she said. "We can talk about Craine later."

Glendon didn't answer but this time it wasn't because he was being ornery. He was already asleep on the floor.

Molly walked wearily to the sofa and lay down. Her stomach grumbled. Except for the hot chocolate, one slice of toast, and half a banana, she'd eaten nothing for thirty-six hours.

As soon as she had a nap, she'd fix something to eat. A bowl of chicken noodle soup would be easy to prepare. She would even eat vegetable soup, if that's all there was.

She closed her eyes. Maybe, she thought sleepily, I'll dream about pizza. Thick, hot pepperoni pizza. With extra cheese.

Minutes later, a siren screamed.

Molly's eyes flew open and she struggled to sit up. For a moment, she thought she was back in Los Angeles, in her own bedroom, hearing a fire truck or a police car in the street below her window.

Buckie barked and she remembered where she was. Had she slept long? She didn't think so but she wasn't sure.

She struggled to her feet. Every inch of her body protested when she moved and she longed to lie back down on the sofa and go to sleep again.

Instead, she walked to a window at the front of the

house and looked out. She gasped and clutched the window ledge.

He was back.

The black pickup truck was roaring down the lane toward the house. The brown llama was still tied in the back.

The siren got louder and she knew it was coming this way. They're after him, she thought. The siren must be a Highway Patrol car or, more likely, the sheriff. Sheriff Donley must be chasing Craine. All she had to do was keep Craine out of the house until the sheriff caught him.

Quickly, she bolted the front door. She ran to the kitchen door and locked it, too.

"What is it?" Glendon asked. "What's happening?"

"It's Craine. He's coming here and I think the sheriff's after him."

Glendon started to get up, moaned, and fell back to the floor. "I can't move," he said.

"You don't have to. Is there any other way he can get in, besides the doors?"

Glendon shook his head, his eyes wide.

Buckie barked again.

Molly's mind whirled. The windows! Was it possible for him to climb in a window? She rushed from window to window, checking each one. They were all tightly fastened.

"Buckie," she called. "Quiet!"

Buckie stopped barking and trotted to Molly's side.

Molly looked at Glendon. "You be quiet, too," she said. "We're going to stay as still as we can and maybe he'll think we aren't here. Maybe he'll try the doors and leave."

Glendon said nothing, but he nodded his head, to show he understood.

Molly put her hand on Buckie's head, trying to calm him so he wouldn't bark again. "Down, Buckie," she whispered, and Buckie lay on the floor in the corner.

The siren was louder now, and she knew it had turned and was coming down the lane toward the house.

Footsteps pounded up the front steps. The door shook. Buckie growled but Molly reached down and stroked his head until he quieted. She stood still, listening.

The siren faded quickly from a loud scream to a thin wail and then quit altogether.

The footsteps thundered off the porch and then, almost immediately, she heard them again, on the back porch. She flattened herself against the kitchen wall and looked down at Glendon. He was still lying on the floor, just inside the kitchen door, with the rug on top of him. He stared back at her and didn't move.

Voices shouted in the front yard. "Around in back!" someone yelled. "You go that way, I'll go this way!"

From where she stood, Molly could see Craine's face

through the glass pane on the back door. He looked desperate, the way an animal might look when it was cornered by hunters. He turned his head from side to side, trying to see if his pursuers had found him. He pounded furiously on the door and Molly wondered if the lock would hold.

She held her breath, hoping he wouldn't look in and see her watching him. Hurry, she pleaded silently to the men. Please, please hurry!

There was a loud crash and glass flew across the kitchen. One big shard hit Molly in the face. Her hand flew to her cheek and when she looked at her fingers, they were red with blood.

Molly looked up again. Craine had put his fist through the glass pane on the back door. Before Molly could react, he reached inside, unlocked the door, and stepped into the kitchen.

As he did, his foot hit Glendon and he looked down. Instantly, he reached down and yanked Glendon to his feet. Glendon cried out but Craine put one arm around Glendon's throat to silence him.

He propelled Glendon out the door and on to the porch. Buckie stood up, growling, but Molly grabbed his harness and held on. She leaned forward, peeking out the door. She knew Craine hadn't seen her.

Sheriff Donley and another man raced around the corners of the house, one from each direction, and stopped. They looked at Glendon and Craine on the porch and then at each other.

"I'm going to get in the truck," Craine said, "and I'm going to drive away. If you want this kid to live, you will stay right where you are and not try to stop me." His left arm was tight around Glendon's throat. His right hand held the gun.

The sheriff and the other man nodded.

But he won't let Glendon live, Molly thought. He's just saying that, so they'll let him get away. He hates Glendon and he'll do something terrible to him.

"Throw your guns on the ground," Craine said.

The two men looked at each other again.

"Now!"

As the sheriff and the other man slowly removed their guns from the holsters, Molly slid her hand across the countertop until she reached the empty mug. She didn't know if she had enough strength left, but it was the only thing she could think of to do. Someone had to stop him. If they let him drive away with Glendon, she was positive she'd never see her cousin alive again.

She grasped the bottom of the mug, looked at her target, and raised her arm. She threw the mug as hard as she could at the back of Craine's head. It hit dead center.

"Hey!" Craine yelled, and instinctively he let go of

Glendon, put both hands to his head, and turned to see what had hit him. Glendon quickly stepped away from him and stumbled across the porch.

Molly let go of Buckie's harness. "Get him!" she screamed and she pointed at Craine. "Get Craine!"

Buckie leaped. With his teeth bared, he flew through the open doorway, straight toward Craine.

At the same instant that Molly yelled at Buckie to get Craine, Sheriff Donley raised his gun and aimed quickly at Craine's legs. Just as Buckie landed on the porch and sank his teeth into Craine's thigh, the sheriff pulled the trigger.

The sound of the gunshot exploded in Molly's ears.

Buckie yelped.

Glendon screamed.

Molly put her face in her hands.

She didn't want to look.

Thirteen

The hospital bed felt wonderful. It was warm and clean and, best of all, safe. At last she could relax, knowing Craine was behind bars.

"There's some mild frostbite in those fingers and toes," the doctor said, "but otherwise you're in remarkably good shape, considering what you've been through. We'll keep you here a day or so, to rest, and then you should be good as new."

"I'm starving," Molly said. "I'm so hungry, I'm even willing to eat cauliflower. And brussels sprouts. And spinach."

Uncle Phil laughed. "That won't be necessary," he said. "We've already ordered soup for you."

"How's Glendon?" Molly asked.

"He's suffering from hypothermia, torn ligaments,

and a broken arm," the doctor said. "They're putting a cast on his arm now and he'll need to stay here in the hospital for a few days, but he should heal nicely. I foresee no complications. You did a nice job with that splint, by the way. He probably would have needed surgery on his arm, if you hadn't held it straight with the spoon."

"Glendon is lucky to be alive," Uncle Phil said. "When the avalanche hit, he covered his head and that must have created an air pocket big enough for him to survive until you dug him out."

Chicken-vegetable soup arrived and Molly thought she'd never tasted anything so delicious. She didn't even bother to pick out the peas. While she ate, Uncle Phil told her what had happened while she and Glendon tried to escape from the avalanche and Craine.

"Karen hovered between life and death all night," he said. "I stayed with her, of course, and I didn't worry about you and Glendon because I got two messages that said Glendon had called and everything at the ranch was fine."

"How is Aunt Karen now?"

"Better. The crisis is over, thank God, and she'll get well. It wasn't poisoning, after all. Your cod-liver-oil pills had a tamperproof seal—the manufacturer can tell from a code number on the label—and the lab found no trace of cyanide or any other poison."

"What was it, then?"

"The cookies."

"*My* cookies? There was poison in the cookies I made?" Molly was horrified. This was even worse than if the cod-liver-oil pills had been at fault. Glendon would hate her for sure, when he heard this.

"Not poison," Uncle Phil said. "Peanuts. Karen is allergic to peanuts and she didn't realize there were any in the cookies. She thought she remembered your mom's recipe."

"There weren't supposed to be peanuts. We didn't have any chocolate chips so I used peanut M & Ms instead."

"Karen couldn't sleep because of her cold, so she got up in the night and made a cup of tea. She decided to have a cookie, too. She said with the raisins and the chocolate, she didn't taste the peanuts right away and she swallowed some. Apparently it triggered a severe asthma attack and she slipped into a coma."

"Just from eating a few peanuts?" Molly was incredulous.

"An allergy to peanuts is not uncommon," the doctor said. "An extreme reaction like this—it's called *anaphylactic shock*—is rare, but it's happened before. Peanut allergy is a strong food allergy."

"I didn't know she was allergic to peanuts," Molly said. "I would never have put them in the cookies, if I'd known."

"There was no way for you to know," Uncle Phil said. "She got a rash from eating peanuts once when she was a child and hasn't eaten any since. I had at least six of those delicious cookies myself, so I should have warned her about the peanuts. I didn't even think about her allergy."

"Neither of you could have guessed she'd have this kind of reaction," the doctor said, "so don't blame yourselves. Just be glad we were able to save her."

Molly finished the soup, closed her eyes, and drifted into sleep. When she awoke, her first thought was that the hospital room would make a terrible collage. Everything was white. She wondered if the administration had ever considered painting all the ceilings red or putting plaid blankets on the beds.

She realized that Sheriff Donley and Uncle Phil were in her room, talking. Apparently their voices had awakened her. She stopped thinking about collages and listened to the conversation.

"How did you know Craine was stealing my llamas?" Uncle Phil asked. "What tipped you off?"

"I got a call from Mort Simmons, a new llama breeder over near Glacier. He said someone from Baldwin Llama Ranch brought in three llamas yesterday, and sold them for less than their value because he needed money fast. The fellow brought a pregnant llama early yesterday morning and returned late in the afternoon with the other two. He had registration papers but Mort wasn't comfortable with Craine's explanation of the background of the animals. He said he had the feeling that Craine didn't really know anything about them."

"I'm surprised Craine used his real name."

"Craine showed him an old business card for Baldwin Llama Ranch, one that still gave his name as a partner. That's what made Mort believe it was a legitimate sale. And he did have the papers for the animals."

Uncle Phil slammed his fist into his palm. "That rat! He knew I keep the registration papers in my file in the barn. All he had to do was match the coloring on the llama to the description on the paper. I don't have any business cards with his name on them, though. I burned those long ago. Do you suppose he saved some cards all this time because he planned to do this?"

Sheriff Donley shrugged. "Business card or not, Mort still felt uneasy about the deal, so this morning he decided to call and ask a few more questions. When he tried to telephone your place, the line was dead. That's when he notified me."

"Thank goodness he did," Uncle Phil said.

"As soon as he said he bought the llamas from Craine, I knew something was wrong," Sheriff Donley said. "My deputy and I headed out to your ranch right away. We had just turned off the Forest Service road onto your lane, when we saw your black truck coming toward us, with a llama tied in the back. Craine was driving."

Molly shifted in bed, listening intently.

"I turned on my siren and blue lights," Sheriff Donley continued, "but instead of pulling over, Craine made a fast U-turn and started back to the ranch."

"Why would he do that?" Uncle Phil said. "The road doesn't go anywhere. He must have known he couldn't escape."

"I suspect he's on some drug and not thinking clearly. I don't know. People like Craine, who break the law, never think they'll be caught and then when they are, they get desperate. He told me in the car on our way to the jail that he would do anything to keep from being locked up again. Anything!"

Uncle Phil shook his head sadly. "Anything except try to earn an honest living," he said. "The saddest part of all this is that Craine wrote to me, just before he got out of prison. He asked me to hire him, to help on the ranch."

"After what happened before?" Sheriff Donley said. "He must be crazy."

"He swore that he'd learned his lesson. He said he'd get $100 when he was discharged and asked me how far I thought he could get with $100 and no job."

"Other people make it. If they want to go straight, they can find work. Don't feel guilty for turning him down."

"I didn't turn him down. I hoped he really had

changed so I offered to let him stay at the ranch with us until he found a job. But he never showed up. After he got out of prison, six weeks ago, I never heard from him. I thought he must have found a job."

"Not Craine," the sheriff said. "He tried to get rich quick by stealing."

"And in the process, he nearly killed my son."

"Your son and your niece. Craine admitted he pushed the bale of hay out of the loft."

"What was he doing in the loft?" Uncle Phil asked. "And why would he want to hurt Molly?"

"He says he only planned to visit you. He hitchhiked as far as he could and then walked the rest of the way to your place. He got there late at night and didn't want to wake you, so he decided to sleep in the barn. He woke up when the ambulance arrived. He saw the attendants put Karen in the ambulance and he saw you leave. That's when he decided he could make some quick money. He'd already seen Merrylegs in the barn and, of course, he knew what she's worth. He figured he could take her away, sell her, and return the truck and you would never know he had been there."

Uncle Phil swore under his breath. "He probably intended all along to steal a llama," he said. "Why else would he carry a gun and come in the middle of the night?"

"Good question. He put Merrylegs on your truck,

parked in the woods until early the next morning, and then drove to Glacier and sold her. Then he brought the truck back and went up in the loft to sleep. He woke up when I arrived to collect the food samples. He thought Glendon had seen him and had called me, so he was furious at Glendon. Later, when he heard someone in the llama pen, he looked down, thought it was Glendon, and shoved the hay over the side." Sheriff Donley ran his fingers through his hair. "Then he climbed down to see if Glendon was still alive and discovered it was Molly instead."

"But why did he bring the truck back?" Uncle Phil asked. "He had the money from Merrylegs; why didn't he keep the truck? Or abandon it somewhere?"

"Greed. It was so easy to sell Merrylegs, and he got so much money, he decided to come back for more llamas."

"Damn him!" Uncle Phil cried. "I should never have answered his letter. I certainly should not have told him how well the ranch was doing and offered to let him stay here while he looked for work." Uncle Phil stood, walked to the window, and gazed out. "All my life, I've been giving him another chance and he always disappoints me. I should have known this wouldn't be any different, even though he gave me that sob story about people on the outside never trusting an ex-con. In his case, he *shouldn't* be trusted. I know that now."

"If you had not offered to help him, and he ended up

in prison again, you'd always blame yourself for not giving him a second chance. Some people *do* change. Some become fine citizens after they're released from prison. You had no way to know if Craine was one of them."

Sheriff Donley turned to Molly. "I owe you an apology," he said. "I assumed the hay incident was accidental. I should have gone up to the loft and looked. I might have found evidence that Craine had been up there. If I had looked around more, perhaps I would even have found Craine, and that would have saved a lot of trouble."

"He had a gun," Uncle Phil said. "If you had looked for him then, we might have had a real tragedy."

"Why does Craine hate Glendon so much?" Molly asked.

"When Craine lived with us," Uncle Phil said, "he was always angry because I spent my spare time with Glendon. Craine wanted me to go fishing and play tennis with him, to do all the things we used to do when we were kids."

Uncle Phil looked sad. "Glendon needed a lot of attention then and when I tried to give it to him, Craine accused me of spoiling him. We argued about it so often that Craine couldn't stand to have Glendon around. To be honest, I think he was jealous."

"Glendon was only four years old," Molly said. "How could a grown man be jealous of a four-year-old?"

"Craine has always had emotional problems. I hoped he'd outgrow them. I thought he would come to his senses and see that he was ruining his life. Unfortunately he never did and now it looks like he never will." Uncle Phil sighed. "I admit Glendon was extremely difficult during that time. But there were reasons for his behavior and Craine should have been more tolerant. Glendon's life hasn't always been easy, Molly. There were problems in the past that you don't know about."

"You mean Gladys?"

Uncle Phil looked astonished. "He told you about Gladys?"

Molly nodded. "And about how his—his mommy left."

"He's never talked about that to anyone. I even took him to a child psychologist, because I knew he had some fears and resentment that he needed help with, but no one could get through to him. He simply refused to discuss it."

Uncle Phil leaned back in his chair, shaking his head in disbelief. "While Craine was with us, Glendon got more and more withdrawn and even after Craine was gone, the problem didn't get better. If I hadn't met Karen, I don't know what would have happened to him. As it is, it was almost a year after Karen and I got married before Glendon accepted her. I know he loves her now and he's been much happier the last couple of years, but even with Karen, he refuses to talk about Gladys and about my divorce. He's kept it bottled up inside himself all this time."

Molly felt honored that Glendon had shared his troubles with her. She knew that it was good for him to talk about Gladys and about how mean his mother had been to him. By talking about it, he could help the pain go away. He could quit dwelling on what happened in the past and put those unhappy years behind him forever.

Sheriff Donley broke into her thoughts. "Mort said you can come and get the llamas any time," he said. "All four of them."

"Four?" Uncle Phil said. "Did Merrylegs have her baby?"

"A healthy little female. Born last night."

"Now that *is* good news," Uncle Phil said.

"Craine was so busy stealing more llamas," the sheriff added, "that he never cashed Mort's checks."

"So there's no money lost," Uncle Phil said.

"Mom isn't going to believe all of this when I write to her," Molly said.

"You won't need to write," Uncle Phil said. "She's catching the first plane home. While the doctor was examining you, your mom called, because she was worried about Karen. When she heard what's happened, she said someone else can introduce the frozen yogurt; she's going to take care of her almost-frozen daughter."

Molly grinned and snuggled deeper under the warm

blankets. Mom was coming home. Everything was going to be all right.

"I guess that means you'll be going home to Los Angeles sooner than you thought," Sheriff Donley said.

"Maybe not," Uncle Phil said. "Molly's mother wants to stay here awhile, to help out until Karen's on her feet again."

Good, Molly thought. Maybe Glendon and I can have some fun together yet. Just two days ago, she would have said the chances of being friends with Glendon were zip. But now that she knew why Glendon had acted the way he did, she was able to forgive him. Besides, they had something in common now; they'd survived an avalanche together.

"My deputy took Buckie to the veterinarian while I booked Craine," Sheriff Donley said. "The vet says the bullet only made a surface wound. He stitched Buckie up and he'll be ready to go home in the morning. You'd better have a good supply of dog food on hand; he's earned it."

"Forget the dog food," Uncle Phil said. "Buckie deserves his favorite treat: macaroni and cheese."

"And a medal for bravery," Molly said.

"I know a certain girl who was brave, too," Uncle Phil said. "If it hadn't been for you, we would have lost Glendon." He leaned over the bed and kissed Molly's cheek.

"Hey!" said a voice from the doorway. "That's my husband you're kissing, young woman."

"Aunt Karen!"

A nurse's aide was pushing Aunt Karen in a wheelchair.

"The doctor said I could be up in the chair for ten minutes. Just long enough to see for myself that my favorite niece is going to be all right."

The aide wheeled Aunt Karen up next to Molly's bed. Aunt Karen took Molly's hand and held it. "Thank goodness you're OK," she said. "When I think how close we came to losing you and Glendon . . ." Her voice trailed off, as if the possibility was too horrible to put into words.

Molly looked at Aunt Karen and Uncle Phil, and saw their love for her shining in their eyes. Maybe tomorrow she'd start a "family collage." She could use denim and red flannel for Uncle Phil's clothes and a pretty pink gingham for Aunt Karen. She'd give Glendon something bright and cheerful, to indicate his new attitude. Yellow, perhaps, or a vivid orange. Maybe she could even find some fake fur and put Buckie in the collage.

"I just came from Glendon's room," Aunt Karen said, "and he said to tell you that when he gets home, he wants to learn the game with Buckie and Fifi. He hopes you'll visit him in the hospital as soon as you can, too. He wondered if you'd like to help him build a model ship."

"Sure," Molly said. "Maybe we can start it tomorrow."

Tomorrow. She smiled sleepily and closed her eyes. Tomorrow Mom would be here. Tomorrow she could leave the hospital and see Merrylegs' new baby. Tomorrow she and Glendon would start being friends.

Tomorrow she might even get pizza for breakfast.

Peg Kehret lives in Washington State, in an old farmhouse surrounded by apple, pear, and plum trees. There is usually a dog at her feet or a cat on her lap as she writes. Music drifts from the barn where her husband, Carl, restores antique player pianos, nickelodeons, and circus calliopes.

In this tranquil, old-fashioned setting, Peg writes fast-paced fiction with enormous appeal for today's young people. Her popular books include *Winning Monologs for Young Actors, Encore!, The Winner,* and *Deadly Stranger.*

She also writes plays for schools and community theaters. Best known are "Spirit!," "Dracula, Darling," and "Bicycles Built for Two." Her plays, which have been produced in all fifty states and Canada, have won numerous awards.